LATE MARRIAGE
PRESS

ABSTRACT

a novel

Sarah D'Stair

**LATE MARRIAGE
PRESS**

First Edition
ISBN: 979-8-3304-2288-3

Published by Late Marriage Press

for Pablo

ABSTRACT

Because of this there is no such thing as one and one.

GERTRUDE STEIN
The Geographical History of America

PART ONE

PART ONE

THE HORRID LITTLE BRAT HAD been staring Cora down all day. Upturned eyes, reddened face, tucked chin and snotty nose, neck turned to look behind her shoulder. She peers back toward some mysterious malefactor, while Cora pretends to look the other way. The girl is mad. No one knows why. Perhaps someone has threatened to take her little dolly. Perhaps her yellow hair has been pulled too tight, or she's just been given a slap for backtalk. Shiny puckered lips and cheeks illuminate a gluttony of white ruffles. A ragged doll, clutched and mangled, looks up at her with fear in its wide eyes. In the background, innocent clouds and a blue sky surround an angry glare of blonde hair.

Cora has despised this little girl for as long as she can remember. They'd see each other on every childhood visit to great-grandmother's house. Cora would walk through the door and there she'd be, every time, just sitting there in silence, always inexplicably mad, always the only face in a dusty collection of trinkets on a table in the living room. The girl's fury had been painted on a decorative plate a long time ago. And why? Cora had often wondered what would possess some unknown painter from the past to emblazon her anguish on a dish for all eternity.

Cora picks up the plate for about the hundredth time. She once again wraps it carefully in paper to prepare it for the moving box, which soon will be full of such artifacts, all the items that pushed great-grandmother's life forward into the grave. She wraps slowly, finds the most tragic newsprint headline to cover the girl's face, to heighten the drama, to give the sniveler something to cry about. Down she goes into the cardboard bed Cora has made for her. And now, what else should go with her? She can't be left there all alone. Maybe the tiny porcelain bowl painted with blue flowers. Or the plastic tulip glued inside a thin green vase. Or at the very least the display stand that's been with her all these years.

Suddenly, and unexpectedly, Cora feels very tired. She slumps for a moment, glances at a piece of paper that carries her task list everywhere it goes. An empty space glares into the room from where the girl once sat with her doll. Cora tries not to stare at the blank outline, forces her eyes away from the table, flitters them back for a moment, tries to put it out of her mind entirely. It's no use. Cora feels another surrender crawl into her lap for a snooze. It doesn't seem right. The phrase "it's no use" echoes through the house, insistent as a mantra. Cora imagines the little girl's anger rising up from the box to smother her in her sleep. She sees the scene captured in twelve-point font: Cora Freelene, 26, strangled last night in the cold grip of a stubborn girl's broken heart. A horrific tantrum fills the house. She can feel it now, welling and shaking, feel it in the pulse of the cat clock hanging on the wall, in the wind outside scratching to come in. Cora needs to let the girl out, out of the box and back into the room that is living.

This is silly, Cora reminds herself. She's not even alive! Still, once again, on the verge of being afraid, Cora unwraps the girl and puts her back where she belongs, the undead come home again to great-grandmother's table. This old, old table, this old, old girl, this wince at the unpacking.

Cora had better get moving. There is no time to lose. It is of the essence! Idioms dance in her mind as she imagines leading a horse to water. She dwells in cliché and grotesque forms of nostalgia, coaxes herself back to the matter at hand. She has been given a task to complete, and a generous time frame in which to complete it. Yet very little progress has been made. Soon, in the scheme of things, grandmother and grandfather will appear in the cracked and tarred driveway and will expect to see all of these lost-to-the-ages trifles packed and boxed and ready to be sold, donated, or thrown in the fiery furnace. Cora's job is to make decisions: to delve, sort, arrange, wrap, pack, and discard thousands of items once in the company of great-grandmother, who is the dearly departed as of a year ago, give or take.

In exchange for sorting and packing, Cora and her cat Chloe have received nearly a year of rent-free suburban living, a veritable gold mine for a twenty-something with a job in the city. Cora and Chloe, against the clock and all odds, will get the job done. That's what they've told themselves, at any rate, yet now it's been almost a full year. Winter, spring steamy summer. All those turns of the hour hand! And still, they have yet to pack a single solitary item. But that's not entirely true. A few stray boxes half full of odds and ends lurk in the hallway and kitchen, but they're packed loose and impermanent, just in case.

Now, after nine months of excuses, the time has come for

Cora to make some choices. If only it were that simple, to declare an organizational triumph and have it be so! At this point, the decisions manifest themselves only in proclamations of Cora's failure. In Cora's mind, however, the problem rests entirely with the little girl, who terrorizes the house as judge and jury, who sees Cora as an escort toward the grave. If only she knew how hopelessly Cora waits for boxes to fill of their own accord, for the stale stench of cardboard to find its way through one of the cracks in the ceiling!

Cora's brooding has brought her all the way to eleven-thirty and her standing date with Judge Jerry Sheindlin at *The People's Court*. Her weekdays end with him, a companion who is always perfectly punctual, reliable, and above all, just. A dusty green tea kettle pours Cora a cup of decaffeinated Earl Grey before she retires to great-grandmother's chair. Its cracked leather lets cotton stuffing make a bristly escape under her legs but luckily, someone has crocheted a pink, blue, and yellow blanket to aid in its concealment. Woolen and itchy from age, the blanket holds tight to its purpose and gives Cora some comfort as she sinks into its crusty folds.

The tense-plodded theme song signals the start of the show, a melody Cora knows like the beat of her own heart. As the show begins, the wall next to her becomes her brief focus, its denuded face robbed of dozens of photographs that used to hang profoundly above great-grandmother's head. Old cousins, second uncles, depression-era rags and stolid smirks, black and white or sepia-toned archives to affirm the family's existence. An over-zealous aunt had already removed them, insisted on their preservation in a padded vault for posterity. Now, above Cora's nightly cup of tea, outlines have replaced storylines, and somewhere, a number of muffled voices long to feel their shapes once again next to great-grandmother's body.

The court cases tonight are marvelously banal. Cora revels in the boredom, savors the minutia of other people's minds, so factual in their concerns, so detailed in their paper trails. Such real life, such pickles gotten into! One woman sues a young man for damages to her vehicle caused by a skateboarding mishap in the grocery store parking lot. She wins her case handily, for the young man could only muster an obvious falsehood. He claims *she* ran into *him*, though damage appears only on the passenger side door. What wonders that man must live! Could he believe it happened that way, truly? Common sense wins the day, as it does in Judge Sheindlin's good hands, and the young man is ordered to pay the woman five hundred and four dollars. Five hundred and four! So wonderfully precise, her calculations. The next case involves a landlord-tenant dispute, a topic rarely of interest to Cora simply because it's often too easy. "Did she pay her rent?" "No." "Is that true? Did you fail to pay your rent?" "Yes." And there you have it. Case closed, open and shut, nothing more to discuss.

The old chair and Cora fade to pastel as Judge Sheindlin departs the bench in a cloud of law and glory. Drowsiness has its own punctuality in this house with great-grandmother's things. Tomorrow will be the day, Cora promises. Tomorrow, all these boxes will fill themselves with immaculate intention.

Cora retires to the back bedroom. Chloe follows. As they fall to sleep, the nearby closet doors spill out shoes and coats, papers and toys and blankets, all of it unused these last thousand years.

THE METRO RIDE TO work is a damaged psyche waiting to be unleashed on the unsuspecting masses. It will never be unleashed; it is hobbled into its tiny doghouse with only two feet of give to the rope, just out of reach of a musty water bowl.

These are Cora's somewhat illogical thoughts on the way to work. The trip is rather short, just a handful of stops down the Red Line, yet time assaults Cora like unruly hands. The metro car shakes and rattles and sways, and Cora is expected by all good folks of society to stay awake despite its scuffling along. An impossible feat in this womb of a train car! She dozes, head heavy against the window, hoping the slight residue from her hair doesn't leave a stain others will notice and give a sneer. The train jolts her awake at every stop, worries her cursory punctuality. Indeed, she has overslept on multiple occasions and missed her stop. Reading, a futile task, only makes her drowsy, gives her mind a reason to drop from the face of the world. Listening to music? Same problem, and besides, Cora is persnickety about music, enjoying so little of it with any real gusto. She often longs for a very large person to take the empty seat next to her, to shrink her own space, to invite her to a party of conscious discomfort when her sleep mouth falls open, her complete lack of self-control on display in the window of a train car. She wants to be shamed into alertness, but it never works. Cora is a snoozy feline, nestled into the crook of a neck.

The journey to work draws to a close in a vast, elaborate

escalator, a kind old usher escorting bodies from the bowels of dim underground to the lighted theater of day. Foolish commuters climb out as if taking the stairs, but Cora allows the device to move her along, infusing her day with a slow crawl, and crispening air, the wobble of a handrail held with mild trepidation. Who knows what filthy-handed tenant has occupied this very spot? Cora gazes up. The concrete symmetry of the tunnel's design provides a break from chaos, a rest from troubled abstraction.

Her destination, a ten-story modern just across from the metro station, meets her each weekday with quiet singularity. She looks toward the top floor, tries to find her own cubicle window, and fails. Once inside, the final leg of the trip requires an elevator ride that opens to a hallway decorated with a windblown skyline at night. Why a picture of night in this place of the day? Cora can fathom the question, but not the answer.

Cora's co-worker and semi-supervisor, Susan, indulges in her daily breakfast and newspaper. Susan fascinates Cora like courtroom participants on television fascinate her, or in a gentle circus-animal kind of way, or like some misshapen classmate you always wanted to kiss just to let them know they are desired, but also won't go near because first of all, you are too shy, and second of all, what do you know about their plights or their ecstasies? Susan smooths her *New York Times* out flat, large and fully splayed on her desk, work papers pushed to the side. Her morning journey begins in the Entertainment section, a slow, methodical read, then moves to the front pages, perused with equal interest, though much less vocal appreciation. She tells Cora about the goings on about town: a new musical depicting civil war in Sudan; a new book about carbohydrates and insomnia; writers from the Middle East who use Western translators to get their work noticed by American literary agents; the final movie of a French director who recently died under suspicious circumstances.

These topics only vaguely interest Cora. However, Susan's enthusiasm could bring Cora to streaming, envious tears. Susan dwells in realms of cultural engagement Cora could never muster for herself. Susan relishes every last article, every day a new wonder, an impermanent drama forgotten by tomorrow's fresh newsprint. Cora is regaled with stories she didn't have to collect herself and will never think about again, like pretty lines in a mediocre stage play that stars your favorite actor. And then, just as methodically with her banana muffin and extra-large coffee, Susan peels the pastry from its wrapping with deliberation, circles it around in her hands, firms it down on the little plate stored at her desk for this very purpose. Each bite is chewed the requisite forty times and ends with a gaping swallow heard by all in the office. The grand coffee cup draws to her lips. She blows faintly into the aperture, slurps rather quietly sip after sip after sip, small and low and ineffectual, waiting for the day's contract to be signed, a court date with an anticipatory throat. Cora watches the dance unfold and listens to the culture section while she gets herself organized for the day.

Susan is the regulatory force of Cora's existence. The slow fingers, slow mouth, the monotone voice of reason so connected to the goings on of the world. Cora eyes Susan with jealousy at the way she keeps track of it all with such freedom of association, such fluency of speech. None of the heaps of detritus that generally fall from Cora's mouth, which chews too quickly, too few times, and can only manage a bit of toast in the morning before work.

The window next to Cora's cubicle mostly looks out on a vast expanse of East Coast trees. But sometimes, when she happens to glance behind her shoulder on a break from typing, an enormous Mormon Temple rises up from the foliage. Its hostile spires evoke the chains of Dante rather than the chains of solemn anchorite priests. Trees and spires. Against this backdrop, and after morning niceties, the job begins.

On a narrow shelf across from the desks rest several book-length bound transcripts of public hearings conducted by both houses of the United States Congress. Their spines are stiff, like outstretched necks, as they wait for someone competent to come along. Cora peruses the titles to decide which subject she would like to populate her day. There are a few Omnibus bills and hearings on the Middle East, but budget issues and foreign affairs have never made their way into her affections. The perusal continues, Cora's head tilted to read with more ease. She needs to choose, but which one calls out to her today?

Finally, the answer finds her. Experientially, she is already engaged as she sees the black letters centered on a volume of about two hundred fifty pages. Its title: *The Rising Price of Quality Postsecondary Education: Fact or Fiction*, a hearing held by the House of Representatives Committee on Education and the Workforce, chaired by the Honorable John

Boehner of Ohio. Envelopes that contain her own monthly student loan bill come to mind and Cora laughs. Fact or fiction? Some glorious human thought of that title! Someone surely who paid nothing from their own pocket for college. Yes, this is the one. She daydreams briefly about infusing cynicism into her work as she anticipates scenes played out on the stage of her own bank account.

The volume's matte cover caresses Cora's hands as she ambles back to her desk. One more sip of coffee, then the ritual opens to the first page. There, as usual, she finds good tidings and performative remarks of politesse, introductions, words of welcome to guests and witnesses, apologies for tardiness or for needing to leave early for a vote on the House floor. This often goes on for a number of pages. Then comes the substance. Statements, testimony, dozens and dozens of appendices with detailed statistical charts and pie graphs and public comments that are most of the time complaints. Cora loves it all, loves the triviality, the grandeur, the triviality disguised as grandeur, loves the hands that had to type and print and bind all of these words together, words that mean nothing and will come to nothing. These words prove one thing: one day some months ago, some very smart people from universities across the land gathered in a room at the Capitol to persuade Congress that higher education is an unwritten social contract, central to the economic health of the nation, crucial to upholding democracy as we know it. A college is a business whose products are human beings, and many of its products are drowning in debt. Cora is enamored of all this life, all these people engaging in such a grand, complex process, one so much bigger than themselves. Look how important all of this seems to those who spoke that day, to those who sent in public comments, to the person adept enough at spreadsheets to make one look so pretty!

Cora is enraptured in the tiny black print, in the feel of smooth paper on her fingers, in the hours it must have taken for these people to act out this drama for no particular reason except to entertain themselves in suit clothes they call their own. The sickly lives tattered between these pages celebrate Cora's meticulous eye for detail. They think she is bringing them to life, that her keystrokes will further mark them indelibly on the historical record.

But that is not Cora's job. Cora's job is not to create, but to destroy.

Cora is an abstractor. She writes abstracts. She must abstract it all out with no remorse. She must examine, condense, cut, excise, truncate, and amend. No word or phrase is safe from her abstraction. Ten pages wither into a neat phrase of ten or fewer words. The next ten are cut altogether. That is Cora's power: to be accurate and inaccurate in equal measure, to blindside irony, to flirt with obfuscation. Some legal clerk or academic researcher of the future will decide the fate of Cora's abstractions. They will read her words uncritically, take them as mere fact, and then decide whether to move their bodies across town to find the full volume on a library shelf. Will it be worth their while? Cora will tell them yes or no.

The process is ugly. It must be so. She reads and loves each word, rolls it around on her tongue to absorb its texture, insists on its significance to trick it, to more cruelly cut it down to size. She keeps phrases tucked in her back pocket to use in place of a thousand: "the benefits for…" and "the effective-ness of…" and "the budgetary restraints impacting…" and dozens of others that she can release to the world at a mo-ment's notice. Monologues are slashed and burned and sliced. She creates to destroy, draws it all into perigee and generali-zation, meaninglessness exists at her beck and call, to the point of futility, meaning brought almost to fissure. All this destruction and no one's the wiser! Hands wet with newsprint, lashes greedy with ink, her fingers type away on a keyboard that is innocently complicit in the crime. Cora is heavenly inside her cubicle, an angel atop a church spire looking down on suitcoats who utter words labeled testimony. Her fingers move from the recesses of thought to the corner margins on a piece of electronic paper. Across the street and over the trees from the Mormon church towers, Cora is busy making art from glorious omission.

Cora buries herself in the text to avoid thinking about the empty cubicle next to her on the left, the one furthest from the window. It's empty because Theresa is not sitting there. She is absent. Only a desk and chair are there instead of her face, which Cora can usually just see over the top of the gray partition. The décor that Cora has chosen for her workday has taken on an air of melancholy. She tries to ignore a line of sight populated by postcards of unvisited European abbeys and castles and old stone bridges.

Theresa starts work at nine o'clock and it is now nine-fifteen. Where is she, and why is she late? Any attempt to investigate would result in a catastrophic revelation of Cora's previous transgression. If she asks Susan, would that give her away? Her sin of desired communion? Her generosity to a fault?

Here's what happened: yesterday Theresa and Cora had gone to lunch together, as they do several times a week. They chose the café downstairs, which sells egg salad Cora likes and a radish salad for Theresa. They are friends, these two. Co-workers but also friends. Theresa would say so, anyway, and so would Cora, to a point, to the point that ends with Theresa's long brown hair curling around the soft curve of her face. And her green eyes hiding like experts behind her glasses. Her solemn voice, a half-smile that always lurks just under her breath. Cora can't help but fixate. Her own eyes conceal a craving, a longing, not in an erotic way, rather like looking at a canvas of insistent pastels that forbid the head from turning away. Theresa's unblemished skin is too much for Cora, the slight pink of her cheeks, the way every anecdote curtains an innocent understanding of the world, one full of families modeled after the television and military-grade older brothers who send postcards to wish the younger sister well. These details inundate. Fascinate. And so, the transgression. And so, the reveal.

It was a bracelet. Nothing fancy at all, rather old-fashioned in a nineteen-seventies sort of way, one might even say retro modern. It was one of the thousands of deliciously ancient items in great-grandmother's house that Cora insists on sharing with the world, though the world may despise them. Just the other day during their lunchtime chat, Theresa had been talking about her admiration for the outfits Janet and Chrissy wore in *Three's Company*. She had wished without humor that she could find clothes that stylish on department store shelves nowadays. In that moment, Cora secretly decided to indulge her lovely friend in some late seventies fashion culled straight from the overstuffed jewelry bin in great-grandmother's bedroom. That night, in a mangled pile of old plastic, Cora had discovered a particularly inimitable piece she thought would appear as the height of passion on Theresa's pale wrist.

Cora brought it to work the next day, which was now yesterday. Why hadn't she handed it over first thing in the morning? A casual gesture? An offhand thought? Why did she wait for lunchtime when it would clearly be kind of a *thing*? An event? Something like a special occasion? It was a blunder, a miscalculation, a careless mistake.

And now, the absence. The gaping injury of Theresa's

empty desk chair draws Cora into the remarks of the Honorable John Boehner. Her calling is to craft the perfect abstract come what may, so she buries herself in the task with gusto, with the bright intensity of a toothache. There is nothing like perfection to drown a wounded conscious mind.

She lasts only a few minutes more before she is willing to risk exposure just to know. She asks Susan, with purposeful inconsequence, if Theresa is coming in today. Susan looks up between enraptured gulps of coffee and says that Theresa had called in sick today, but will likely return tomorrow. This is all the evidence Cora needs. She has committed the unspeakable crime of sharing herself, of tempting consequence with great-grandmother's fashion paraphernalia. She has told herself many times to be wary of such actions, swearing up and down she will never again assume others' good intentions. Yet each time the opportunity arises, Cora simply can't help herself. She gives in. Sometimes, she simply must make a mistake.

AFTER WORK CORA DECIDES to get Chinese take-out, despite knowing she will eat only a small portion then throw the rest away. An indulgence perhaps, but great-grand-mother's kitchen is not suitable for cooking, and certainly the refrigerator would render leftovers unpalatable even after its cursory clean-out a few days after the death. Cora unleashes wastefulness on great-grandmother's house, which retaliates by dirtying everything it touches.

Cora's meticulousness rescues the best bits of Mongolian beef from an overindulgence of onions while she lounges with Chloe on the living room couch. She contemplates her appre-ciation for whomever invented the foot-powered trash can lid and realizes that tonight is the night to tackle the kitchen. It's the perfect time for a Holy War against grime, the ancient re-gime of grease stains and coffee mugs strewn about the cabi-nets alongside old tins of waxing paste and jars of used cook-ing oil. Tonight she will make some progress, or at least main-tain a perfected distraction from other ills she is nursing. Bed-room jewelry. Living rooms denuded of faces. She gives Chloe a pet on her way to the garbage can now loaded with half-eaten menu items from around town.

Kitchen gloves seem a sensible option, but Cora resists. If great-grandmother could live here happily then so can she.

This logic lasts until an encounter with the first and most tender item on the counter waiting to be boxed. It's the flesh and blood of an old electric bowl mixer, a languishing gem emblazoned with the phrase Merry Maid on the side. The green of the bowl and body of the machine have faded to a yellowed sickness, the steel mixer blades now a rusted muscle of kitchenware innovation. And there, with full irony, are the words Merry Maid stamped into the next millennium.

Cora's hand touches the bowl and dances with decades of dirt and grease. Cora herself yellows to the point of nausea. Another decision must be made: to continue the sickly task, or to fashion the perennial fork in the road. Maybe this all can wait. Maybe we should let the maid see a little more light of day before the interment. Or perhaps what they all need is some good mood music, to make the job merry, to render Cora herself a merry maid in great-grandmother's decrepit house. Delighted at the many ways she can belabor a phrase, Cora makes her way toward the record albums at rest near the dusty record player. After shuffling through a few, Al Martino's "Spanish Eyes" casts away indecision and excites the perimeter of Cora's imagination. Swollen, crooning, velvet-voiced patriarchy, love and a dirty kitchen-aid. Martino's voice fumigates the air.

Cora returns to her task, which now is a large drawer sticky with age and disuse. Inside, treasures of antique store kitchenalia: a metallic blue ice cream scoop, a hand mixer with rust for blades, whisks of all sizes in various stages of mangling, ancient cheese graters, spatulas missing their handles, pizza cutters crusted with red sauce, an oddly clean soup ladle, two pasta strainers, and at least a hundred cookie cutters in shapes that fit precisely into Euclid's appetite. In short, a wonderland. Cora can't wait to dive in, to immerse her hands in utility and discovered joy. She will place each item in a box without care or discernment. They all must continue their existence somewhere outside of great-grandmother's kitchen, and Cora must say where. To auction? To the landfill? To the keep pile? But for whom to keep? And how shall she decide? Cora is confronted with futility. An object's worth assigned at random, regardless of great-grandmother's skin cells still clinging to the plastic. Sentimentality in the ring with arthritic hands. Cora can't think what to do.

She lifts a single burn-sided spatula out of the drawer and places it in the garbage can to the side of the refrigerator.

There it lay, solitary and quiet, just atop the greasy Chinese food bag. Forlorn. Melancholy without its counterparts. After so many years of in-drawer solidarity, dormant but together, it comes to this? The blackened thing lay like a child in the tomb of a grownup. Cora is an undertaker, undertaker of the undead.

She can't bear to look at it, can't bring herself to close the garbage lid. A softness falls in the kitchen air. Now is not the time. She lifts the poor thing out of its doom and places it back in the drawer. Maybe tomorrow she will be able to make the leap. Maybe tomorrow. The drawer closes and the weepy thing is out of sight. Relief and impotence mingle with Martino's serenade. Cora must get something done. And tonight. She must, at least before Judge Sheindlin. That will be the deadline, a race against time and the television. Who will prevail? Cora, or her lacking?

In a search for absolution, she surveys the room for some begging object, some over-burdened utensil calling to be put out of sight. Which of you *wants* to be boxed? She listens to the room knowing she listens to nothing. Her turning eye catches some lonely looking mixing bowls lost in their own nostalgia. Cooking smells, cake mixes, children's hands, perhaps even her own. All of them are lost. These bowls are brown faded to yellow, sweet white flowers wrap around their middles like a young girl's delicate flower chain. They fit, the five, into each other. They have been together their whole lives, from factory floor all the way to great-grandmother's kitchen table. This table, indifferent to style but still modern in its yellow-glittered retro flair, is marred only by an apathetic coating of grime. If nothing else, it'll serve as a firm foundation for nested bowls readying themselves for travel.

Just as Cora places a box onto the table, Chloe, always keen for an empty box, jumps up and nestles herself squarely inside its corners. She wants to play. Cora can't resist, so they play. Cora lays her hand flat to Chloe's tummy, then traces her fingers around the rim of the box until Chloe jumps out, paws at the pounce. The hand disappears only to crawl back up toward Chloe's inevitable attack, hand to tummy, hand around box, pounce, paw, bite, over and over until Chloe nibbles her own foot in distraction. Cora draws her back into the game with a pat on the tummy, and then again Chloe is on the hunt for Cora and her hand, her willing prey. The fun lasts several minutes, after which Chloe, bored or thirsty, jumps down and wanders into the next room.

Cora realizes her time is not infinite. She also knows that haste is a reliable remedy for wasted time, so the yellowed bowls find themselves tossed haphazardly into the box, unwrapped, untidied, unprepared for their future rough journey. She places the box on the floor behind the sparkly table, an unfinished task hidden from sight. A bother to no one, now, and Cora has also therefore packed something tonight! No one can deny that. She has won. She is the victor!

Al Martino's stretch on the record player has ended. And now, silence. The bratty girl laughs at Cora for leaving the kitchen unfinished, for stopping before she even began. A new plan formulates in Cora's mind while Chloe needles at her feet. Tomorrow, the following kitchen items will be wrapped, boxed, and prepared for donation: a sixteen-piece set of delicate China; twenty teacups with saucers; a serving tray shaped like companion seashells; three butter dishes; twenty or thirty stained coffee cups; a dozen glass tumblers; and a set of measuring cups hanging from a nail on the wall. It will be a triumph altogether!

Cora roams the house ghost-like in the quiet looking for tasks to add to her list. Silence lives on this side of the equation, loneliness on the other. Cora looks out across the equal sign but she can't see that far away. Great-grandmother's house is suspended in unlit space, a darkness no sound can escape. The record player cannot rescue her from the heavy air, nor can the television. Cora and Chloe are alone.

In great-grandmother's bedroom, the hometown of the offending bracelet, a jewelry case holds hundreds of mournful rings in a dresser drawer that hangs open like a gaping mouth. All these mottled, unfingered rings repulse even themselves. Cora picks one up to disturb the peace. A bright ruby on a tarnished silver band clings to her middle finger. Cora holds her hand out to be kissed by some invisible lover, sits on the edge of the dusty, unmade bed, and wonders why a person cannot complete a single task while in these rooms and hallways.

ON THE METRO RIDE to work Cora can't stop thinking about the ruling Judge Sheindlin had to make last night. Two owners, two claims, one dog. It was a landlord-tenant case in-

volving abandoned property, only instead of a mattress or dining table or clothes, the disputed item was an adorable Pomeranian. After the tenant moved and left the dog behind, the
landlord's family took the dog in and became quite attached.
For three months they cared for the dog and loved her, and
now, the former tenant wants her back. Sheindlin had to make
a tough call. In the end, the dog was returned to the irresponsible young tenant. Justice had *not* been served.

To add to her woes, all the window seats on the metro were
taken this morning. No head rest means Cora must try extra
diligently to stay awake. Despite her best efforts, her head
drops occasionally without permission, the dog's fate disturb-
ing her half dreams until her neck tenses reliably back into
place. In waking moments, unruly memories of Theresa's
apartment mingle with the frightened face of the Pomeranian
huddled under courtroom lights. She had been there once, to
Theresa's apartment, for pizza and a movie. If it were anyone
else's house, the event would have halted at the invitation
stage. Socially inept Cora, after all, could never have decided
what to wear. The familiar scene would play itself out: dozens
of outfits tried and judged and discarded in a heap on the floor,
disgust on the face in the mirror, countless failed attempts to

get out the door. At times, already in the car with the ignition turned, she would remove the key and return to her despairing closet doors to run through the stage play once again. Cora is not one to accept invitations. The consequences are too severe. But this was Theresa. Friend, colleague, lunch associate, cubicle neighbor, partner in gossip and lighthearted ridicule. Theresa has taken a seat within a very small circle of people around whom Cora can wear any old thing with impunity.

The film they watched that night stars Reese Witherspoon as a wealthy young woman from California who goes to Harvard Law, wears pink, outsmarts a scummy big shot lawyer, and gets engaged to Anthony from *Bottle Rocket*. Theresa and Cora, on the floor near an empty pizza box and bottles of Coca Cola, enjoy the young woman's victory over a man. What was the name of that movie? Cora's sleepy senses can't quite remember the title, though it definitely lurks somewhere in the file folder of fond memories. She allows herself, for a moment, to wonder if Theresa would be at work today. And if not, what could be done in response. Would she ask Susan again at risk of exposing her desperation? Offer a casual mention to colleagues to see what they know? Or in the extreme, dare to call Theresa on the telephone? Paralysis claims the very thought. All of it, doubtful. Cora is stymied by her own destination, her own failure to advance.

An absence called Theresa's desk greets her as she walks toward her workspace. No worries yet, it's not yet nine o'clock. One can still hope, and in fact, it's ridiculous to assume her friend would quit without notice simply because Cora gave her an ugly piece of plastic on a whim one day at lunch. On the other hand, though, Theresa is rather young, and doesn't need the money, and has a loving family who would support her. As she's said a number of times, this job is merely for early career resume building, so anything is possible.

Susan is talking about the news again, world events at the moment. She says something about Pakistan, but an empty coffee mug renders Cora a pathetic listener. At some point between newsprint phrases, Cora will wander to the break room. She will choose her moment wisely, find the exhale where Pakistan holds a pause, and take her leave. She will be quick with her return, then she'll get right to work. Coffee and sugar will escort her into the Senate chamber.

A colleague named Julie disorders the corridor on the way to the break room. Julie is Cora's other work friend, an indexer. On the whole, she is suffered more than relished. She cannot organize herself or her papers, yet has the nerve to extend Cora repeated invitations to her basement apartment in Adams Morgan. Cora is obliged to stop by her cubicle to say Hello. The hem of Julie's forest-green skirt lay on the ground waiting to be wrapped around the wheels of the chair. An oversized scarf hides a slender neck but indulges in the bulky disregard of her torso. Flat black sandals, no socks, brown hair loose in a ponytail down her back. She is the paragon of unkempt beauty. She talks about nothing with vigor, coerces significance out of each syllable. Julie can get things done. She is an activist, a pot smoker, an habitual incense burner, an indexer of Cora's abstracts. Cora recognizes the scent of Julie's apartment in the air of her cubicle, a far cry from great-grandmother's dust and Chloe's morsels in gravy.

Julie's inanity distracts Cora from the disheartening absence that waits for her back at her desk. Julie and her verbosity meet Cora's monosyllabic responses, cordial smile, staccato deceit. Their talk is of the new CEO of the company, a political rally held downtown over the weekend, a party Julie went to with her activist friends. Cora simply wants to get her coffee.

After ten minutes, Cora is safely back in front of her computer, surrounded by the sound of Susan and the silence of Theresa. She dives into a new hearing transcript for the day, and is vaguely interested despite being disorientated by some of the technical jargon. "Transition to Digital Television" is presided over by Senator John McCain of Arizona, Chairman of the Senate Committee on Commerce, Science, and Transportation. This particular committee is getting a bit too big for its britches. How can one single group of senators handle all of that? But then again, what does Cora know about the calculus performed in the highest levels of government? Her job is to abstract. It isn't to judge.

Despite the empty chair, she tries to pay attention, at least enough to summarize, to quash a purpose, to fragment multitudes and to omit subtlety. Cora seeks magical phrase work, which must originate in comprehension. She tries and fails to comprehend. Tries again, fails again. Words organize themselves in straight lines for the length of a paragraph. And for what purpose? Merely to expose an incongruent mind? John McCain's eloquence, his clear, convincing speech indulges Cora's distraction. At least a dozen sentences that once fell from the Senator's mouth become blank repetitions. The words lose their referents. Signifier minus signified equals Cora's desperation.

She finally discards distraction enough to grasp a bit of what they're saying. A change in television viewing is afoot: the government has given several large corporations carte blanche and a blank check to ensure that at least eighty-five percent of American consumers have access to high-definition television. Cora wonders what that could mean. High-definition television. Is it a clearer image? A bigger screen? Something like 3-D reaching out to grab us in our living rooms? And why? Would Judge Sheindlin's face appear even more glorious and wise and handsome in high definition? Would it make him any more appealing to Cora, more punctual, more just?

These meanderings entertain Cora for a few minutes before the clock again centers the frame. The time is nine-thirty, and still no Theresa. She doesn't mention this miniature drama taking place on the stage of the next desk over. Not to Susan, not to anyone. Not even an air of disinterest crosses her furled eyebrows which are now buried deep in the crevices of the text. After all, perhaps Theresa is simply running late, no worries, just a metro train delay or extra heavy traffic. Court is in recess until ten o'clock, after which all bets are off. Cora will then play both judge and jury, cast in the role to convict both herself and Theresa. Herself for the audacity of giving a gift. Theresa for the crime of heartbreak. She must withhold judgement for now, though, and turn her thoughts back to John McCain's television.

By lunchtime Cora is sure Theresa will never speak to her again, as sure as she is that someday something called HDTV will force its way into millions of unsuspecting living rooms, as sure as she misses the Judge Wapner of her youth. The task now, though, is to remedy her pathetic lack of a lunch partner. Who will fill the void? Julie would definitely accompany her, but can she endure Julie for a full hour today? Social action and the squeak of rubber sandals on the way to a sandwich shop? And what if Julie wants to eat Thai or Indian instead of the egg salad downstairs? Cora must revisit the point of origin without noisy shoes and a floppy ponytail.

After a few more deliberations, she remembers Adam. They hadn't spoken since the day many weeks ago, maybe even many months, when he asked her to play golf with him sometime. Golf? Cora hardly knew what to say, so she said nothing and had avoided him ever since. Adam. A nice guy, fun to have as a friend during boring meetings about increasing automation or the reorganization that may one day cost us our jobs. A reasonable conversationalist, for the most part, though he believes himself much more interesting than he should. Yes, Adam will do for lunch today, a perfect solution to the problem. Cora will put him to use as an exemplar of her standard operating procedure. She slinks over to his cubicle just down the hall in the opposite direction from Julie. She asks him, Do you have any lunch plans? We haven't chatted in weeks, so much to catch up on. Cora looks to the side and contemplates the efficacy of certain kinds of blather.

Adam agrees to the lunch invitation, as expected. It is the only course of action for such an amenable fellow. And of course the sandwich shop sounds great. Anything Cora wants.

Downstairs, the café table begs for Theresa as Cora takes a seat and looks around, hoping her friend will somehow enter the scene. No luck. Meanwhile, conversation with Adam reeks of forgetting and tongue-in-cheek irritation. The tragedy of the Bush presidency, Congressional ineptitude, the educational-industrial complex, all with a child's dose of humor. It's better than Julie's desperate seriousness, but still, Cora simply doesn't care. Cora's true genius is in pretending to care, but today, in the face of things, even her ability to parrot her favorite NPR commentators has left her in the cold. And what remains? What remains, obviously, are Adam's eyebrows. Thick and dark, they move along the y axis to the rhythm of his talking jaw. Yes, those are the distraction Cora needs. Magnificent and repulsive, their eminence will save Cora from a wasteland of mindful wanderings during her break from John McCain.

LEGALLY BLONDE. THE TITLE of the movie had come to her on the way home from work in a moment she wasn't even thinking of Theresa. A silly film, really, but the two had enjoyed it, laughing at the compunction of the protagonist, feeling minimally inspired to take charge of their own lives. Theresa abstracted the film: beautiful young woman struggles to be taken seriously. Nothing profound, but the phrasing was economical enough.

Cora wants to watch the film again. The reason feels compelling, though enigmatic. Her car seems to drive itself from the metro station to the independent video store just down the street from great-grandmother's house. What exactly causes her to pull into the strip mall parking lot without question, fully intent on renting a copy of the video? Why does she look first through the window of the martial arts studio next door to Potomac Video and watch children practice their kicks? How does she eventually walk through the door, shudder past the children's section replete with local mother holding a copy of *Arthur's Baby*, ignore the annoying posters for *Blow Up* and *Bottle Shock*, two movies she swears never to see, enter the comedy section alphabetized by title, and rest her eyes immediately on the film she would like to see? What force quickens her hand to flick it from the shelf? Cora's favorite questions are the ones with no answers. A quick investigation of the VHS tape shows it had been rented often, but looks in good enough repair to work for her purposes.

A tiny porn room huddles like a scared kitten at the far end of the shop, its size mere estimation for Cora has not been inside. Each store visit elicits at least one momentary thought of going in, and sometimes she even looks in the room's direction. However, shyness bars the door. A young woman alone looking at pornography? That might be some other person's style, but it is not Cora's. Besides, even if she gathered enough strength to rent some salacious title or another, great-grand-mother's house is no place for sexual activity. In that house, desire runs perpendicular to broken teacups.

Careful not to appear inconsiderate of the attendant's valu-able time, Cora approaches the counter already reaching for her wallet. Besides, she needs to hurry and get home to Chloe. As her eyes trail toward checkout, Cora realizes the store em-ployee is someone she hasn't seen here before. She frequents the store enough to know he must be new. A twinge of anxiety leads the way as she, undeterred, makes her way to him.

He doesn't stand upon her arrival, hardly seems to notice her, doesn't even look up, in fact, until she places the video tape firmly on the counter. He had been perched at the other end typing on a large laptop computer plugged into the wall, typing and typing while peering into the screen. Cora inter-rupts his white button-down shirt and dark framed glasses and lovely pale skin and crouched shoulders, stops them in their tracks. She wants to know what he is typing, and more than that, wants to know what could possibly be more engaging than her desire to hand him two dollars and fifty cents to take this VHS tape out of the store.

His eyes leave the screen a second or two before his finger-tips. A deep, sonorous voice surprises the room with "I'll be right with you" just as he types his last sentence. His height matches Cora's disquiet as he stands, tall and grand, to step toward the register. This is the man that will know the secrets of her movie rental history. His investigation wouldn't reveal a completely terrible record, but she does tend to owe late fees on the silliest of films. She once owed fifteen dollars for *The Full Monty* and twenty for *Anne of Green Gables* after about a dozen melancholy views.

The unsuspecting video tape lay alone on the counter. It sends an illegible telegraph that if deciphered would spell out the terms of Cora's embarrassment. An unaccompanied mi-nor, it searches for counterweight in a film by Godard or Fel-lini or Jarmusch. How will this man know that Cora is much more intelligent than her current rental choice might indicate? Although he hardly seems to care, hardly seems to notice her at all. Typical, she remarks to herself, of someone who couldn't bother to leave his computer until the last second, who seems to avoid all eye contact, and who, in the entire transaction, says only a few utilitarian phrases in her direction. His perfunctory politesse does not impress her. That will be two dollars and fifty-nine cents, he says. Pitiable opening salvo.

Cora is incensed and ashamed, irritated with this rented video she doesn't even like. Just because of him, she may never set foot in this establishment again! Before she skulks away, she offers him a Thank you while looking directly at his face and eyeglasses. He doesn't accept the challenge. The click and clack of the keyboard punctuates her departure, distracts her footsteps all the way out to the car.

CHLOE GREETS CORA AS she walks in the door with a preternatural sense for when her friend will return. And then, Cora's favorite, the reunion ritual. Chloe won't settle until Cora picks her up, the two cheek to cheek and nose to nose, the entire universe in statis until Chloe has had her fill. Intimacy this precise happens only with Cora and cats. And how could it be otherwise? How distasteful would it be for some man or woman to wait at the door for attention, follow her from room to room, sit on the bathroom rug while she showers, sit with her in great-grandmother's chair? Cora and Chloe exist together in perfect symmetry, a blissful peace in which nothing is asked that cannot be given.

Cora's eye catches the rented VHS tape on top of the television and she calculates the probability that she will ever watch it. All numbers are irrational tonight. Besides, there's so much to do in the kitchen! It needs to be a work night; she must finish what she started. After a cursory change into house clothes, Cora's decision about mood music becomes the first order of business. A particularly well-loved album by Robert Goulet raises its hand from the top of the pile, so Cora calls him out. Yes, old friend, your crooning can participate in the evening. A little peanut butter and jelly prepares her for the work at hand while Goulet turnstiles the room.

All things considered her to-do list *is* rather long. The first concise bullet point tells her to pack up fifty years' worth of someone else's living. Cora has so far failed at the task, but tonight? Tonight will be the night for success. Perhaps she should choose objects more ancillary to actual living, artifacts lurking in unopened cabinets and bottom drawers. Perhaps then she could make progress. Like an archeologist with her fossils, she will re-write the stages of history.

A quick scan of the kitchen reveals a floor cabinet next to the refrigerator that reaches out toward Cora in loneliness. She grabs one of the larger boxes and some newspapers in preparation for whatever may be languishing inside. It turns out to be several oversized serving dishes more appropriate for the manor house than great-grandmother's cottage peasantry. However, it's entirely possible that great-grandmother had a different life altogether before Cora knew her.

The first item seems to have been clear crystal at some point, but now looks an oily mess. Cora has unearthed an enormous punch bowl with twelve crystal hooks around the rim to hang serving cups. Twelve hooks. What grandeur! Two serving cups have been resting in the bowl for decades, but the others have been scattered like forgotten remains. She finds eleven total, but despite her best efforts, the twelfth, separated from its siblings, must have been lost. A casualty, perhaps, of a careless hand or a raucous partygoer. Unable to bear the labor of individually wrapping each piece, Cora places all eleven cups inside the bowl and heaves the whole apparatus as gently as possible into the box.

Cora dives back in, hands and arms submerged in the cabinet's dark recesses to feel her way toward the next item. Her fingers embrace the grime as she pulls out a yellow-green serving tray shaped like a dubious sombrero. Hideous. And resplendent. She imagines sundresses on summer afternoons while Goulet bellows in the background. Where will this sickly abomination find love? Surely someone must have loved it once. Now, its fate is left to Cora's imagination, which can find no better solution than wrapping it tight in paper and hiding it away.

The house has taken its toll for the night even though it's only been thirty minutes. The thought of opening more cabinets gives way to fatigue and a general sense that oil and dirt are traveling up Cora's arms and into her hair and face. Grime has won the war; nothing can continue without a shower. She can finish the kitchen on the weekend when she has more time.

Cora wonders on the way to the bathroom what Reese Witherspoon would look like in high definition. No image comes to mind. She gives Chloe a pat on the head and resolves, from this point on, to pay more attention to what the Senators are saying. No distractions, no shifting eyes, no long conversations. Just work, Chloe, and great-grandmother's house. The grandparents expect it to be completed in the time allotted, which, thanks to the skin of filth that now covers Cora's body, is unlikely. A feeling of guilt follows her into the shower. Surely her disgust would be an insult to great-grandmother. If it weren't for Chloe curled up on the bathroom rug and the hot water over her face, Cora wouldn't know what to do.

The end point of a shower always requires lengthy consideration. Cora is happy to oblige. Maybe it's the strength of gravity in a porcelain tub, or maybe the steam subdues her thoughts just enough to find a moment of calm. Searching for reasons to leave seems a futile effort against the Napoleon strength of hot water. Just as Cora begins to seriously consider turning off the water to continue the evening, a large mole on her stomach comes into focus. Assured by doctors all her life that it's a benign structure, Cora nevertheless worries. It's rather loose on its hinges tonight, one might almost say hanging by a thread. Come to think of it, she had felt earlier a bit of waistline discomfort at the point of contact, but thought nothing of it at the time. She gives a diagnostic brush of her fingertip to the spot, the result of which is now a mole languishing in her hand instead of on her body. Blood descends in a silky stream along her belly, competing with streaks of water for space along Cora's skin. What does one do with a mole torn from the body by accident? Let it go down the drain? Throw it in the garbage? The whole thing seems absurd, and a little scary.

She reaches for a cup on the sink counter and puts the mole inside. Attention must now be turned to the glisten of blood all down the front of her body. The water proves an ineffective deterrent so Cora decides she must at last turn off the shower and see if any bandages can be found in great-grandmother's house. Blood ruins a light blue towel during her search, which comes up empty. Having no other recourse, Cora folds up some tissues and tapes them to her body using a small piece of packing tape. She will need to find a band-aid first thing tomorrow, if she lasts that long, she thinks, with all this blood.

The tissues seem to do the trick, as far as Cora can tell, and the evening's activities have left her with tape irritating her skin and a mole idling in a cup on great-grandmother's bathroom counter. Robert Goulet's voice has faded and the record has stopped. Cora sits in the dilapidated chair with Chloe and waits for Judge Sheindlin to bring an end to the day.

PART TWO

PART TWO

THERESA HAS BEEN GONE a week with no explanation. According to Susan, she may not even return. Hurricane Cora has made landfall, a swirl of confusion battering the peninsula. Several times over the past few days, a call on the telephone seemed a logical move, a simple phone call to check on a friend's health and well-being. It would be a reasonable thing to do. Yet each time Cora imagines her fingers dialing the number, she is met first with mistrust, then with terror. Theresa undoubtedly feels disgust at Cora's impertinence.

A pale grey conference room now houses Cora along with several members of the legal editing staff. A plush office chair, comfortable in its way, suffers through a manager's extensive speeches. Facts and figures project themselves onto color-coded spreadsheets: subscription rates, company workflows, the impending disaster of automation. It's unclear if this last point is true or simply a scare tactic to get employees to work harder. Either way, Cora begins to daydream about pleasanter things. Like the wisp of hair Theresa pulled in nonchalance from her own mouth on the way to the bookstore, and the windy day that brought the miracle to pass. Cora relinquishes herself to hopeless meanderings, but only on condition of a strict five-minute time limit, which happens to be as long as it will take for the manager to finish talking about profit-loss margins typical of a mid-size publisher.

Several weeks ago during an unsuspecting lunch hour, Cora and Theresa had wandered to the large bookshop just down the street, a chain store affair replete with café dining and a marvelously tucked-away escalator to the second and third floors. Roaming the genre fiction section, Theresa had mentioned that mysteries are the only books she can finish, the only ones that don't bore her. At the time, Cora found this trait intolerable, anti-intellectual, and overall quite off-putting. However, today, in a conference room dreaming of cozy mysteries and *A is for Alibi*, she finds it utterly enchanting. Cora has a way with the past.

Cora looks around to see who is left in her life. Adam and his eyebrows nod as if the boss in the blue shirt speaks directly to him. He asks a question to illustrate his solid engagement with activities of upper management. An unappealing trait, this fervor, especially after Adam's tirade against this very lecturer just the other day. The blue-shirted voice sends sound waves across the curved space of Cora's desk chair, entirely unaware of her disdain. Susan is in the room, along with another abstractor named Ron, who has a sticky face and greasy grey hair. Nausea defines itself by the odor of his body. Across the table, a few others have joined the ranks, none of whom have been caught in the net of Cora's friendship.

And then Julie, who seems as bored as Cora, though perhaps better at masking it. A deep maroon blouse and black flowing skirt almost obscure her more annoying qualities, her endless voice, her activist tendencies, a vague association with incense. Cora can see only one side of her face, which seems almost transparent under fluorescent office lighting. Soft, childlike in its lack of imperfection. Julie is a constant, attractive in her way, unchanging in how she offers hope for Cora to keep two feet on the ground. Past, present, and future converge into memories of Chloe as Cora wonders how much cat hair is visible on her black shirt. Tonight, great-grandmother's knick-knackery will distract her from these musings, but now, she and the room long for Theresa's perfume.

After the meeting, Cora works on a particularly pesky abstract during the last hour before lunch. Perfect words have eluded her since yesterday, but now it really must get done. The Senate Committee on Environment and Public Works, considering an amendment to legislation from nineteen-eighty, wants to clean up something called "brownfields," the definition of which includes the phrase "lightly contaminated." Essentially, toxic waste dumps. They are searching for a decontamination plan suitable to both industry and environmental groups. At least that's what they say is their goal. But truly, can anyone be trusted? Lightly contaminated. Such a productive phrase! Cora's thoughts enter the darkness under great-grandmother's kitchen sink.

At lunchtime, Cora decides to travel to the lightly contaminated bookstore. Maybe there will be some old novel that will hold her interest for the metro ride home, or some book on the physics of black holes she will read with enthusiasm but not understand. Maybe Theresa will be there. She does live in the area so it's not an impossibility. Before she leaves the building, Cora performs for the bathroom mirror a quick check of lips and face.

People on the street tend to walk in pairs. How easy life

must be for them! There they are, striding alongside a physicality, nonfiction atoms in the shape of a body on Wisconsin Avenue. These are the real mysteries, as strange as sunspots or ten-dimensional space.

The bookstore genre section navigates Cora's boredom. Monotone colors line the shelves—bright pink romance, reddened mystery, dark grey science fiction. Last pages are haunted by inappropriate yawns. What's the use of reading a book that gives a summary of itself at the end? Does anyone really care who did the crime anyway? Or who finds amorous affection? She tries to read a page from a random mystery but can hardly stomach her own disinterest. What could Theresa possibly see in these?

She might as well get a coffee instead. Cora turns her back on the genre section and makes her way down the escalator to the café. All through the store, books are off kilter, out of sync with their stacks, slightly askew or in the wrong place entirely. Compulsion is in the air. Cora tidies the stacks as she passes, puts the tables in order, her lightly contaminated hand exerts control. Before she arrives where she plans to relax, the whole place suddenly becomes a bore. Coffee, a bore. Piles of books, a bore. Even the disorganized handcart by the customer service desk, nothing but a bore. The walk back to work, a bore. Traffic sounds, a bore, and all the busy pedestrians. Her abstract, in the light of day, is also a bore, and rather brooding in all its talk of toxicity. Cora wonders if she will ever watch the VHS tape presently collecting dust and late fees. Perhaps she will take the time tonight if nothing else strikes her interest.

CHLOE IS IN A desperate state when Cora gets home. The day had been a ruthless bully, tormenting her with Cora's absence. Cora holds Chloe tight to her chest. Chloe responds with a growling purr and effusive whisker nudges to Cora's glasses, possessive love bestowed on an object that Chloe thinks is part of Cora's face.

After the hugs and assurances and promises that she would stay home the rest of the night, Cora spends some time flinging Chloe's favorite hair band around the house. The lonely cat becomes a ravaging hunter as Chloe stalks and prepares to pounce. Her keen eye follows the toy as it flies across the room, then she takes off at super speed, claws to the carpet in aid of propulsion, stopping short just before making contact. She catwalks away to feign disinterest, then finds the closest hiding spot to watch it fly across the room once again. This is Cora and Chloe's favorite game.

Once the fun is over, Cora changes into her comfy clothes and gets down to business. It's the kitchen again tonight, the top shelf in one of the corner cabinets she had opened several times before but couldn't bear the thought of cleaning. Determination will save the day, for Cora had come home from work invigorated, ready to tackle all manner of tasks.

Upon inspection, the upper-class cabinet reveals great-grandmother's unsurprising affinity for cookie jars. How many are necessary to constitute a collection? Cora counts five. Not enough for a museum shelf, but certainly more than reside in the average kitchen. Cookie jars, grotesque in their exponential rotundity, laugh in Cora's face as she reaches tip-toe on a pedestal. The first is a massive clown with a belly bulging in bright red pants. His white gloves hold his over-large middle, which protrudes circular, almost as if thrusting his pelvis into Cora's groping hands. His smile creeps along underneath painted nostrils, the narrative arc of a nightmare. Next to him for all these decades sits the clown's bodily inverse. Another clown, but with an absurdly slender stomach that elaborates his ballooned pants. Supernaturally ballooned, like stolen masses of helium. Cora places the two on the countertop and tries to avoid the creeps. Next is a jolly round cat with white painted ear hair and wide, innocent eyes. Its head comes off for the cookies. Cora can't decide if the cat is unsettling or if the room is filled with scary clown residue. Maybe a bit of both. She decides to keep the cat jar for herself just to spite it.

Cora peers far back into the darkest part of the cabinet, quiet and still and hidden. Vague outlines almost reach her field of vision of animals sitting there in the dark. A sturdy stepstool and hard countertop support Cora's grasping as her fingertips brush the two figures closer and closer toward the shelf's edge. Two matching puppy dogs appear, ugly at first, dirty white with brown smudges of paint all over for fur. Their large, heavy ceramic bodies resist efforts to pull them out into the light, but Cora prevails. The two dog-shaped faces peer out with human eyes and perfect black eyebrows, decorative flourishes that, whether accidental or on purpose, indicate a somewhat deranged creator. Sitting dog-like on their haunches, the sweet and hideous pair wait for Cora's next move. They must be brothers, identical twins born from the back-alley of great-grandmother's kitchen.

Cora reaches high up on her tiptoes to grab the first, which she plans to wrap gently in paper with his sibling. These two must be worth something. How could it be otherwise?

She grasps its paw with a nudge to the end of the shelf just at the same time as Chloe chooses to continue her hairband antics across the room. One second of distraction and the heavy jar slips down right onto Cora's steadying hand on the counter. Gravity italicizes the moment, a brilliant keystroke em-dashes Cora's two fingers before they can reasonably run for cover. After such precise contact, the ceramic puppy topples to the ground with a crack. Sound rises, spirits fall. To Cora's horror, the thing has shattered into at least half a dozen pieces.

Barbra Streisand's *Funny Girl* plays songs on the record player to remind Cora of the remaining cookie jar. They had made it, these two, for decades together until Cora entered their lives. She purposefully avoids the human-looking eyes peering down at her, though the evasion will haunt her for the rest of the evening. Two throbbing fingers and one dog-shaped jar plunge themselves into a well of pity, lapping and drowning and coming up for air. Perhaps she can glue the dog back together, restore time to its former self. Perhaps all will be well again, then. But she must face facts. It's no use. It's simply too broken, too cracked from the hard fall. There is nothing to be done. Cora exhales the length of a one-inch margin, then places the ceramic fragments on the counter.

She shifts attention to her two fingers, bruised now along the tips and fingernails. Yet another wound to manage, just when her bleeding stomach was starting to heal. Just her luck. Cora gives Chloe a pat with her good hand on the way to the bathroom. Some cool water will hopefully deaden the increasing sharp pain. She flicks the record player to 'off' just at the start of "Don't Rain on My Parade."

Over the sound of running sink water, the bratty girl snickers from across the house. From all the way across the house! The laughter has become a regular occurrence, and Cora doesn't like it. The girl deserves one thing: to be smashed. Unmendable, silenced. Cora's softest footsteps make their way down the hall to the living room. Will she still be there, or has she moved somehow? Even a slight inch or two? Two and a half decades of expectation disregard great-grandmother's choice of decor. Still there, same spot, same smirk, same blond hair, same dusty tabletop, same television VHS, same boxes, same cracked leather chair, same hollow outlines on the same pale green wall.

If only Cora hadn't agreed to do this job in the first place. The whole thing is simply annoying. She hardly even knew great-grandmother, never even knew why they all called her Ralph. It couldn't possibly be her name. How annoying that they called her that! How annoying that Cora's fingers hurt, that she'll need to deal with broken shards of a cookie jar!

Cora wants to go to bed now, even before Judge Sheindlin. Bruised fingers and a decimated puppy, work life a complication impossible to condense. Even she couldn't capture in a ten-word phrase the walk to the back bedroom, the overwhelming empathy for every closed door in the house. Great-grandmother, an unknown quantity, a mathematical identity with zero as sum. Cora erases lines on a piece of paper where great-grandmother showed her work. Mercilessly, melancholically. Quiet and trembling, like the bed where she slept for fifty years after her husband died. Is it great-grandmother's sadness or her own that Cora presently feels? She can hardly tell. Perhaps she will sort it out tomorrow. Best to leave that door closed for now despite the dim light shining from underneath.

Chloe's playfulness comes to the rescue, as it often does.

She jumps under the covers as Cora makes the bed, waits for a hidden hand to inch toward her from overtop. Once again, Cora plays the prey, fingertips closing in on Chloe's waiting paws and mouth, which are less powerful from under the blanket. After a few minutes of fierce attack, Chloe slinks out from hiding and curls up on Cora's pillow. Cora likes to take the corner that's left. Chloe's purr remedies the depth of Cora's solitude as she tells the house good night.

CORA'S FINGERS HURT QUITE badly the next day. Her swollen index finger and darkened purple nail pecks at the keyboard in execution of her job. The middle finger suffers less from the assault, but still, bruised and beaten, it is very little use. The brownfields hearing has to rely on Cora's other fingers, which distract from the experience of abstraction. It would only happen once, being abstracted, and for its turn, it has to endure a mutilation. No fair. The others got ninety words per minute.

Cora's mind drifts again to Theresa. Should she call just to make sure her friend is okay? Perhaps even a brief conversation would lend a clue as to the timing of her departure, her future plans, her current feelings toward the events of several days ago. If only she could get some news, Cora promises never to cross the line again. No one would even have to know! She could call from the private meeting room, out of earshot. It could be their secret if that's what Theresa wants. No problem at all, Cora will take good care. A secret, a secret. A secret! An innocuous transgression. A mild offense. A trespass. A contravention, at the least. Sometimes even a crime! All of this, even after Cora promised never to cross the line!

Cora and her abandoned plan look to Susan for help. Information lurks on the other side of the cubicle wall. Cora is sure of it. But maybe Susan is unable to give Cora what she wants. Or unwilling! And she would be right. Who knows what Cora would do with such information? It's best that she keeps it to herself. Or maybe the silence is at Theresa's command. Maybe Cora has been exposed this whole time without even knowing! She looks up to see if Susan is looking. Can she hear Cora's heart pound out its panic and shame? A bruised finger pulses to the rhythm of a flushed neck and face.

As Cora's attention falls on the ache in her typing fingers, Julie surreptitiously enters the scene. Theresa's desk chair is none the wiser. The stage is crowded and claustrophobic, sad postcards on the wall shudder beyond their borders. Cora turns away from the keyboard to find Julie's body filling the space just behind her. The invasion, the blood circulating with intention in Cora's fingers. Why is this happening? Hopefully, the tidiness of Cora's cubicle will repel her, perfect piles of paper, a clean coffee cup, files organized alphabetically and by type.

Julie talks fast, asks about plans for the weekend. It's Friday and they are young in the city. Apparently, those two facts put together means that Cora must have plans. She does, she says. She's going to clean great-grandmother's house. A deadline looms, and there is still so much to do. Julie is unconvinced by this reasoned, if evasive, logic. Cora should come out after work, meet a few friends at this bar down the street. Just for happy hour. Surely she has time enough for such a diminutive gathering.

Cora desires the melodic resonance of No, to hear aloud: No, that will not happen in my lifetime. However, her voice must have received a different message. Before she can intervene, Cora hears herself say aloud: Sure, that sounds like fun.

Julie leaves satisfied, but Cora is a wreck. Who is that

woman anyway, to think she can enter Cora's space with impunity? This cube is sacred, solitary, purposefully tucked in the office corner, populated with papers and pens touched by one hand only. The alarm bell rings from just down the hall and it is the sound of Julie's laughter. How can she laugh, or sleep at night? Does she not know that Cora only enters others' spaces, not the other way around? That way, she can disengage at any moment. There are brownfields all around.

Let's reason this out, configure a plan and test its feasibility. Excuses might be hiding in the crevices and need a little coaxing to come out. Cora checks between all the cracks in her fractured subconscious but finds only darkness. Another viable option: she could back out, plain and simple. But then there will be questions with no answers and Cora likes to keep those for herself. Who are these so-called friends, anyway? Will Cora have anything at all to say to them? And what is she wearing? Ah yes, this old shirt. Sorry old shirt, for springing this on you. Sorry, old pants. Slovenly, unattractive Cora. Why did she say yes?

All these worries culminate in Theresa's chair and great-grandmother's queen-size bed. Stillness, a visionary silence. Is that Cora's future, to be voided from existence, too? Isn't she allowed, even for an afternoon, to be like other people, to engage in conversation, to commune effortlessly in a room capitalized for such a purpose?

Yes, she is allowed. She will go. She will talk to these people with confidence and charm. They will love her without even knowing why! Her old shirt's feelings will be put to the side along with Chloe's extra hours of loneliness. It's Friday after all, a day for preemptive promises. I promise, faraway Chloe, to stay home the whole rest of the weekend.

Productivity rescues Cora from too much dread. The brownfields hearing finally finds its footing in a seventy-two-word abstract perfectly aligned to the margin's edge all the way down. The admiration ritual lasts ten minutes instead of the usual thirty, unfortunate for the brownfields but Cora must put all that to the side for now. She will mourn its loss later. Next on her list, a rather short hearing, hardly worth all these people's time, she imagines. E-signing documents in the financial industry, what a boon! A prophetic innovation, a time-saver in the extreme. Hands to pen and paper? Who can stomach such a thing at the dawn of the millennium? Hyperbole attacks unsuspecting black text and gives Cora a slight headache. Suspicious. Millions of dotted lines lurk under zeros and ones, a game of hide-and-seek with imaginary legal obligations. Electronic autographs dot the i's of Cora's preoccupation.

The abstract is rather easy to write. Nothing complicated. Five o-clock arrives just as the last un-inked phrase appears on the computer screen. Time for this event to get itself over with.

Cora's small backpack encumbers the walk to the bar down the street. Coffee mug, uneaten weekday snacks, a couple of books to pretend to read on the metro, all of it clings to her body with a slight bounce to the beat of her footsteps. Julie is talking again, this time insisting that Cora will really like all these friends of hers. She met them during a stint as an organizer of human rights campaigns in the D.C. metro area. The very fact is all Julie needs. The simplicity of this method of organization interests Cora much more than their activism. By the next minute of the walk, Cora is bored already, though she would never say so. And remember, she has decided to be charming and utterly irresistible this afternoon.

The restaurant, noisy with music Cora has never heard and would prefer never to hear again, is full of people with feet tethered to the ground. How can they all understand each other? Shouted conversations mute the possibility that actual words will be exchanged. Cora is in orbit looking down on earth wondering how they continue to be alive.

At some point in the turbulence, they all seem to have planned a weekend getaway to Newport, Rhode Island where Julie's parents live. Cora makes out some phrases about the parents' humble lives. They don't live in a seaside mansion. They are working class people, Julie assures the table, who live in a small four-bedroom home a few blocks from the sea.

One woman with long curly hair cajoles Cora to join them on the trip. Another man with a tucked-in shirt and shaggy beard joins in her insistence. Cora says she'll think about it. The words do a good job of hiding her intentions, but just then, unexpectedly a hand and shoulder come together in a way that feels mildly flirtatious. Julie's hand. Cora's shoulder. What does one feel about this sudden turn of events? Annoyance, for a start, at being left out of the loop on such a thing. Cora would have appreciated an interoffice memo on the subject before she agreed to sit at a crowded table with this woman. Cora, imprisoned, notices that Julie has more words to say about nothing than Cora would have about the whole of campaign finance reform, about which she had just learned a great deal from a rather lengthy congressional hearing on the subject. Was that one John McCain, too? Cora can't remember. The hour feels more and more adrift as it passes, though Cora manages to hold her own in conversation. She counts her successes in moments of laughter as she regales the strangers with tales about great-grandmother's house, Chloe's proclivities, the tragic cookie jar accident. The stories behave as if they have nothing to do with her. It's not their fault. All these smiles egg them on, encourage them to violate their parole, urge them on toward improvisation in defiance of mother's protests.

Julie calls intermission with an abrupt question about Theresa's whereabouts. Do you know anything, Cora? Perfection in the curved spine of the question mark. Has she told you anything? No, I haven't heard anything. Have you? No, nothing.

Julie knows nothing. What a precious bit of information, worth the entire afternoon!

Theresa's absence remains a mystery to everyone. Cora hasn't been singularly excluded at all. What a relief! At the same time, what else could be the cause if not the overture toward further friendship, the gift culled from the depths of great-grandmother's bracelet bin? As the din continues around her, Cora renews her vow never to give a gift again.

Six o'clock rescues the evening's protagonist from the noise of human activity. Cora stares out the metro car window the entire ride back to her station, contemplating what she will eat for dinner, anticipating the warmth of Chloe's hugs, wondering how she'll get by without the firm regularity of work to keep great-grandmother's belongings from gobbling her up. The video store clerk who ignored her with such panache vaguely comes into focus. He has perfected the art of disregard to the point of genius. Admirable trickery! Somehow he has kept himself on her mind, almost every idle moment sees him standing there. Always taller than expected. Curious, the way he leans so far over the keyboard. The way his index fingers take the lead. But who takes a computer with them to work? His obvious intelligence covers a multitude of sins, renders insignificant his inferior words per minute.

As her car begins its short journey from the station to great-grandmother's house, Cora gets the feeling things are out of her control. Instead of a left, the car takes a right. Did she even use her blinker? She just wants to see if he's there, that's all.

She could drive by the video store window, innocuous, anonymous. She could peer in at just the right angle and get a glimpse of the person behind the counter. Just a glimpse. She may return the dusty video tape this weekend if Chloe allows it, but for now, just a peek will suffice.

After three passes by the storefront, Cora settles into his absence. A young female employee stands in his place, a girl she has seen there before. No sign of his white button-down shirt or laptop computer. At least not where she could see. Maybe she should go inside, find a movie to keep her company over the weekend. Something she's already seen but could play over and over for sounds other than great-grandmother's crooning records. The car pulls into a spot, but only briefly. She decides instead to get home to Chloe, who by now must be in a panic that Cora has been gone so long.

GREAT-GRANDMOTHER'S HOUSE WRAPS around Cora's fatigue. She sleeps late, nose and throat heavy with the damp air of the back bedroom. Chloe lay on the little blanket bed next to Cora's feet, as always. The day is already hot and bright. Noise from the window air conditioning unit hums to the tune of Cora's misfortune, allows her racing thoughts to take center stage in the crowded theatre.

This crisp new day, yes, will send it all to the back of the line. A list forms on the dented pillow. Theresa's disappearance, Julie's advanced invitations, the threat of a sudden visit by the grandparents, unfinished tasks, empty boxes, her still aching fingers. Cora's clarified mind will play the match game with the sunny day, turn over the cards of progress.

Tucked way back at the other end of the hall, the third bedroom decides to test Cora's resolve. The worst room in the house. An image appears from the corner margins, a memory from almost a year ago when she first began the process of cleaning. The door had been opened once, briefly, to size the place up. Paper and paper and paper and more paper. Pale magazines and sick newspapers, coupon mailers, envelopes, greying bookshelves filled with books without readers. Multiplication accumulates fewer numbers than infinity and both accumulate less than great-grandmother's third bedroom. It was once an office, or so it appears, with handmade filing boxes and a sagging wooden desk. At some point, paper trails must have triumphed, taken over, populated the new world exponentially over time. No e-signatures here. Only the fall of a meticulously ordered civilization.

Over coffee, plans begin to emerge. The counterattack must be precise, no room for doubt. Immediately, Cora apologizes for using the word 'attack.' The house needs constant appeasement, otherwise who knows what it might unleash on her or innocent Chloe? Let's say, the organizational methodology must be precise. Yes, that sounds better. How will she go about re-arranging items in the room? That is the question at hand. Though she doesn't want to say it aloud, Cora knows that most, if not all, of the papers will simply need to be thrown away. Yet there may be treasures buried under some of the piles – original birth certificates, marriage licenses, who knows, maybe even an old will to turn the family topsy turvy. In one hand, careful consideration, in the other, a large black garbage bag.

Cora throws away a couple of ten-year-old TV guides, along with some yellowed grocery store mailers. Her refusal to look inside either publication is a testament to her determination not to procrastinate. It was delightfully easy to declare those first few items rubbish. The envelopes, however, are a bit more intimidating. They stand tall in stacks all across the room like the origins of Picasso's staircase. Cora imagines the room lit by pale candlelight, like a wizened old corner in a Dickens novel. Sorry to ruin its hard-fought aesthetic, she offers an apology as she picks up the first envelope.

The paper inside is dated October 15, 1985. A medical bill of some sort, perhaps for some routine lab work, something of that sort. Such a wonderfully mundane piece of paper! How could such a profound tribute to the minute reality of human experience simply be tossed in this unromantic garbage bag? The solution becomes clear. What Cora needs is more space. Space to organize, to categorize, to sift and collate and assemble. Papers will naturally sort themselves by type. Cora's job is simply to listen, and to be the legs that carry them. Linnean classification to the rescue! Once so arranged, decisions about their future will be a cinch.

But where would these piles go? Cora steps out into the hallway to commune with providence. The hallway. Perfect. All this free real estate stretches almost the length of the house. The stacks would practically line themselves up! Cora sets dutifully to work, each old piece of paper refining the geometry of her imagination.

After a dozen or so envelopes nestle themselves neatly in the hall, the quiet begins to intrude. It's all Cora can hear. How could she forget the music? Music is always needed in great-grandmother's house. Some kind of noise to wrestle with melancholy so it leaves Cora alone. Off she goes to the album collection in the living room. The perusal this time leads her right into the arms of Frankie Laine, no doubt a superstar in great-grandmother's time but an unknown quantity in Cora's. He is handsome enough in that nineteen-fifties way, a time when symmetry had no hold on the popular consciousness. Surely the music would redeem his sagging cheekbones and creepy smile. *That's My Desire* seems an auspicious title, hopeful even, with a dash of wistfulness, fitting for the task at hand. The big band saxophone and jazzy deep voice of Mr. Laine make even the papers seem to dance in their piles.

Cora Methodical is her given name today. A landing strip forms the length of the hall leaving room for Cora and Chloe to walk. Along the sides, congruent shapes recall pictures of base times height drawn on childhood chalkboards. Mortgage statements, utility bills, tax notices, Medicare pamphlets, uncashed social security checks in trifling amounts, insurance claims, appliance repair receipts, user manuals, property tax forms dating back decades, coupon mailers, shopping catalogs, cards and notes from friends and family, scrawled lists and reminders. Piles soon extend to a second row and Cora is making progress. She ferries credit card statements and aged grocery lists, sometimes two and three at a time, installing them with their counterparts, a reunion of strangers at the hands of Cora's exuberance.

The third bedroom and its vast collection is being thinned with each passing minute, all to the tune of Frankie Laine's velveteen voice. "To hear you whisper low just when it's time to go...." Cora thinks about very little the entire afternoon, except during brief pauses to reset the needle when the album plays itself out. Background lyrics, supermarket coupons. "I get along very well without you" serenades lawn care receipts and requests for charity funds. Half-written recipes on crisp paper find their way into old Frankie's "Someday you will seek me and will find me." When piles get too high, a new one forms nearby, careful to conform to established patterns. Cora tiptoes as the hallway fills with retirement brochures and bank statements, palaces of paper built to faded tunes of nineteen-fifties romance.

After a solid hour of re-arranging, Chloe arrives at stage right, her delayed entrance a surprise even to Cora. How could Cora forget that Chloe was sleeping just in the next room? Keep your eyes on the ball, Cora! Don't lose sight of anything or you will lose it all. Thankfully, Chloe hasn't disappeared despite Cora's preoccupation.

Chloe sits square on a pile of rectangles. Her weight topples the stack, which seems to give her pleasure. Chloe quickly realizes the vast playground Cora has created, and she begins to play. A huntress stalking prey on the savannah, Chloe hides behind one tower then pounces on another. She tucks her nose under one envelope while striking another with the force of her tail. She revels in the playhouse, a dynamo on the hallway stage with ears pricked and head darting side to side. Cora attempts to explain with logic and clarity that a job needs to get done, that Chloe's shenanigans are impeding progress. But Chloe is simply having too much fun.

Cora's attempts to nudge Chloe away from the highest stacks of paper soon become part of the game. The two chase each other down the hall, Chloe hiding just long enough to jump out when she thinks Cora isn't looking. The piles suffer. The organizational pattern scoffs and jeers. It's worth it. Cora can always tidy the mess once Chloe has exhausted herself. The two play for almost thirty minutes, after which Cora, in a brilliant bit of subterfuge, distracts Chloe with some tuna in the kitchen.

Cora sorts into the evening, now and then re-defining patterns for Chloe's participation. Piles and piles of paper line the hallway, and still many, many more clutter the room. What could Cora do overnight to preserve the headway from Chloe's boredom? What a shame if tomorrow is spent re-surfacing the pavement of today. An idea forms from the depths of great-grandmother's crowded linen closet. Towels. Great-grandmother has hundreds of them. Cora decides to place long strips of bath towels along the hallway over top of the papers, which she would then remove in the morning in hopes that the papers would have been protected from Chloe's nighttime bar-hopping. A fine plan. One accomplishment among many today. The towel closet spills out its graphic aids, and Cora arranges them like algebraic line segments. Simple and complex, with end points of equal measure, the work will rest until tomorrow, another long weekend day, when the third bedroom assignment will be perfected and ready to turn in to teacher.

CORA WAKES THE NEXT morning to the word 'excruciating' in Times New Roman on the page. Her fingers hurt. The black and blue fingers wonder what will become of them-selves, how they will type all day tomorrow without being driven crazy. Hunting and pecking just isn't their style after so many years of j-y-j j-y-j. They hardly know how to type incorrectly. Sleepy on her pillow, Cora considers a visit to the doctor, but immediately chastises the idea for its extrava-gance.

Chloe bounces around the house as if she genuinely missed Cora overnight, though she slept right next to her. The morn-ing plod to the coffee machine is greeted with a pounce from under the living room table, a nip at the legs when Cora doesn't offer at least a pat as she passes by. Cora is never sure what motivates Chloe's chipper morning demeanor. Is it gen-uine, or a manipulation for quicker access to morsels and gravy? It doesn't really matter. Sunday morning joy bouncing toward her food bowl has no regard for motivation or the dis-comfort in Cora's fingers and hand.

Yesterday was productive, but still, the back room is a mess. The length of the hallway, covered with papers, appears di-sheveled despite Cora's attempts to preserve order. Even her favorite breakfast of coffee and Cheerios can't quite put things right. Another long workday. Cora is determined, after a

shower and more coffee, to finish the room, clear out the hallway, and perhaps even return the video tape in time to avoid
further late fees.

Heaps of paper in the third bedroom seemed to have grown
overnight. They continue to gain stature even as Cora begins
to remove them! Corners and closet floors, fecund with futility, laugh at Cora's diligence. She can hear them snicker. To
give herself a short break from their mockery, and also because she is running out of room in the hallway, Cora decides
to look more closely at the books that have accumulated on
the bookshelf. She clears a path, trying to remember if she had
ever seen great-grandmother with a book in her hand. No, she
can't remember. There's no explanation for their presence.
They must have appeared solely for Cora's amusement, random novels and hobby manuals, children's books, a number
of old maps held vertically between coffee table tomes.

Cora uses her good hand to pull down a book about marbles.
Two hundred fifty pages of marbles. Pictures, historical information, identification tips, price comparisons. Did someone
in the family collect marbles? Cora hadn't seen any jars of
marbles in great-grandmother's house. Half a dozen books inform readers about various bird species of North America.

Trout fishing in the Western United States. A travel guide to Montana. Cross-stich techniques. Easy Italian recipes. Model train identification. Great-grandmother, the polymath!

The term 'useless' begins to simmer in Cora's mind, a bother of a word. Can there be a useless book? Useless knowledge? Outdated, useless - synonyms, cousins, both? Surely great-grandmother's bookshelf asks all the right questions. Cora searches the spines for answers but finds only more boxes she cannot fill. Her mind drifts to her own books, currently nestled in boxes and boxes and boxes within a storage facility. They wait patiently for her to resume her actual life, for her to understand all their meanings once again. Her hands and her eyes. Her turns of pages, the texture of her fingertips undoing their sad silence. Their words undoing hers.

Just before Cora can put these thoughts out to pasture, an octagonal picture frame comes into focus. It hangs close to the bookshelf, hiding itself from most angles of the room. The shape announces itself as Stop, an uncanny yet appropriate sentiment given the trajectory of Cora's contemplations.

A small filing cabinet stands in the way of a closer look, so Cora scoots it aside. The house in the painting intrigues her.

She wants to peer inside but is thwarted by its mere two dimensions. From where she'd been standing, the house seemed old and charming and quaint; however, up close, like reverse impressionism, she sees only dilapidation. Neglect. Wooden slats that beg for paint, a roof with paltry thatches. Sepia-toned gloom hints at the end of Autumn, the greying brown hues of winter. The whole place is almost too heavy for itself, too many years have passed it by. In the foreground, two old-fashioned milk pails lay on their sides, empty, unhappy with disuse.

Above the house in painted letters is the phase "The LORD takes pleasure in them that fear him." Curious, from a grammatical standpoint. Shouldn't it be 'those' instead of 'them'? Cora allows the phrase to ruminate, checks it against rules of language both learned and internalized. Yes, it should definitely be 'those that fear'. Undoubtedly. So what gives? Cora can't help but smile in slight ridicule, the lord herself on judgement day. Grammatical dialect aside, the sentiment is rather grim. The lord is pleased by their fear. Were these people smote, then, milk pails and thatching left for dead? Had they too little fear, too little trembling, too little self-denial for the lord's indulgence? The windows are too dark, the house too empty. Cora still cannot see inside. An ominous pall shadows the day, casts itself over Cora's organizational system. The demonstrative, awkward in its error, the sense of dissolution, the prohibitive shape of it all. Cora decides to take a break from her endeavors to see how Chloe is spending her time.

As soon as Cora turns to leave, her present circumstances return to focus. The musty room, the endless printed ink, the drab grey walls. The room suddenly seems very small and Cora very large. And then there's Chloe. She has installed herself on the carpet just where one ray of sunlight peeks through shuttered blinds. Chloe stares at Cora with a blank look, nothing particular to say. Cora is trapped. Playing with Chloe means staying here, no antidote for the creepiness, no solution to these increasingly uncooperative pieces of paper. This room now seems as haunted as great-grandmother's bed, waiting to consume Cora to nothing.

Chloe admonishes her friend to get something done. It's mid-morning on a Sunday, Chloe says, and all you've done is stare at the wall. You're right, Cora responds. You're right! It is time, you are right. Back to work. Productivity is key. Make today like yesterday.

Cora searches for some new way to regulate the mess, to consolidate and prepare for eventual decisions about what stays and what goes. She looks around, deflated. In the corner of the room, a bright red ribbon peeks out from underneath some envelopes. Shy red ribbon, embarrassed at being the only color in the house. The package unearthed is a group of postcards, old, dingy, carefully wrapped together. Perhaps evidence of some secret tryst, or a long-lost overseas pen pal! Families have secrets. Her maternal grandmother, for example, once had an affair with a female artist. No one knew until the funeral when the artist herself showed up and told the story. Secrets are really just people living their lives.

Unwrapped, the cards reveal themselves to be less than imagined. Easter cards, brief holiday greetings at Christmastime, all from various unknown east coasters who obviously knew of great-grandmother. A number of apologies for failing to visit, so many excuses. A sick dog, a child's sports tournament, a generic use of the word 'hectic'. Overall, fairly banal. Mundane. Evidence of uneventful years spent in due diligence with family and friend correspondence.

A number of the postcards are blank. Clearly purchased for

some purpose that had gone unrealized. Paris, Florence, Assisi, the Eiffel Tower, the Uffizi. Great-grandmother must have visited these places. Perhaps she simply enjoyed the pictures, never meant to send them at all. Perhaps, like Cora, she merely wanted a place for her daydreams to live.

Many of the cards are not as exotic as these European landmarks. Quotidian scenes from middle-class American life pose as travel destinations, mid-century picket fences, Cadillacs, brothers and sisters riding bikes on tree-lined suburban streets. One shows an overhead image of a public swimming pool, wading white bodies scattered in blue water and lifeguards dutifully at their stations. It has that nineteen-sixties quality of being somewhere between photograph and painting. Staged, but real. All of it a paragon. An ordinary day at the pool rendered exemplar.

Its oddness gives Cora a brilliant idea. Theresa would love this strange relic. Perhaps she'd want to hang it on her refrigerator, or find a frame to fit it to her wall, a curio to deepen her apartment's eclectic décor, to add to the endless trinkets emblematic of life's adventures thus far. Yes, this postcard needs to fulfill its purpose. Its purpose is Theresa. An old-fashioned snail mail sentiment matching great-grandmother's collection of bromides now unwrapped from a deliberate red bow. A caring, but not too caring note just to let her know she is thought of formally by a friend and colleague. Nothing of import. No thought put into the message. Thought would ruin the whole idea. Short and sweet. Cora finds a pen that works on great-grandmother's desk, jots the words without concern for neatness or eloquence. "Susan told me you were ill. Thinking of you. Hope you get well soon." What a risk Cora has taken! To write the original without a draft, especially on such a one-of-a-kind picture! She hopes Theresa finds the message inane, dull, unfitting for what she knows of Cora's personality and way with words. A perfect, innocuous plan. She will place the card in the mail tomorrow morning.

AS ALWAYS, CORA IS late for work the next morning. She never identifies as a tardy person, yet still, she's almost always late. Time simply sneaks up on her, gluttonous in its disregard for her ambitions. Responsible plans to eat a healthy breakfast and walk before work seem silly in retrospect. Instead, she runs out the door with barely a bowl of cereal to hold her until lunch, only having time to give Chloe a cursory pat on the head. A truly pathetic showing for a Monday morning, the first day of Chloe's long, lonely week.

The postcard will need to be dropped in the mail after work rather than before. Typical. Although the delay does give her options. The mailbox near the grocery store has a later pickup time, and fortuitously, also happens to be near the video store. Perhaps the new clerk will menace her with aloofness. Perhaps she'll even rent a movie. Or maybe she'll simply drive by stalker-like once again. She can decide later. For now, she must navigate the perilous day at work, where Julie will certainly ask for more of her attention.

Susan is full of the morning news again. She asks Cora if she's following investigations into the USS Cole. Cora admits she is not. No one can really know what happened and why, so what's the point? 'Informed' is a smokescreen. An illusion. An abstract at best. Cora finds endless ways to justify self-absorption. She may even be right; however, considering her audience, she puts these thoughts on mute.

The ship bombing a dead end, Susan turns her monologue to the weekend, to stories involving garden mulch, trips to Home Depot, and a picnic that went terribly wrong when her twelve-year-old son threw a tantrum in the park. Susan's stories of parenthood make Cora never want to have children.

Today's hearing choices, paltry and few in number, insulate Cora against too much thinking. A few omnibus budget bills, hefty in size but not in substance, the electricity crisis in California, aviation industry regulation. Electricity is boring. Airplanes are boring. Ships and cars, too. All modes of transportation bore Cora to tears, especially when senators and experts discuss them with an air of romanticism. Settling on a comparable bore, Cora flicks the hearing from the shelf and returns to her desk to dig in. The job must be done, after all. Glumly or with joy, either way, the abstract must come forth.

Proclaimed in capital letters on the front page of her choice are the words "Domestic Response Capabilities for Terrorism Involving Weapons of Mass Destruction." The title wants to intimidate, but it's no match for Cora's capacity for deflection. She spends several minutes enjoying the niceties transcribed on the first few pages. The Committee chairman, John Kyle, senator from Arizona, apologizes for being late. There were three simultaneous votes on the Senate floor, which delayed the party luncheons, which in turn delayed the hearing. Magnificent! What are these party luncheons? What is served?

Who hobnobs with whom and how? Do they change their clothes for lunch, then return to their offices for a quick change before Committee work resumes? Such backstage secrets! Political theatre, staged theater, it's all the same. Cora imagines Senator Boxer in a teal-green sequined party dress.

A few pages in, Cora's eyes glaze over. State-sponsored terrorism, nuclear warfare, biological weapons, some fellow named Bin Laden. All of it should be riveting, terrifying, but Cora would much rather collect intelligence about Theresa's mysterious departure. Casting disinterest aside, and being a professional, Cora eventually manages to find linguistic economy appropriate for such important affairs. She writes at least twenty eight-to-ten-word phrases, all before lunch, all despite busted fingers!

Interrupting the admiration phase, a snappy What did you do this weekend? greets Cora from around the corner. Julie. Beaming. Annoying. Earlier in the day, mid-morning, Cora had seen Julie's cubicle empty and hoped all day to catch a break. No luck. What did Cora do this weekend? Throw a hairband around for Chloe, move some papers around, peer into a video store window? Could she say any of that? What an intrusive question! Cora mumbles a quiet Not Much, and then allows Julie to talk. Julie never does Not Much with her weekend. A party in Georgetown, a fundraising dinner for human rights, a date with a woman who ended up being a Republican. Julie couldn't bear to finish out the meal with this woman, it seems. Cora tries to get interested but can't.

How are your fingers? The question is abrupt. Cora isn't prepared. What had Cora told her? The truth? Or had she lied and doesn't remember? Or had Julie happened to see the bandages just now and so asked out of immediate concern? To be safe, Cora simply says, They're fine, healing, but still sore. It's not exactly the truth. One finger turns darker by the hour and Cora can hardly manage basic tasks without discomfort. Julie wants a They're fine, though, so Cora satisfies her.

The next set of questions proves just as aggressive: Do you want to go out next weekend? Maybe Friday night, take it easy, dinner and a movie, my place? What can Cora say? She is speechless, absent of thought in the face of it, unwilling to say what might be said. Yeah, sounds like fun. The answer echoes into the world from the hollow core of Cora's self-awareness. And to add to it: I need a break from my great-grandmother's house anyway. Need a break? Who is saying this?

Julie is happy. Cora panics, sure of two things: first, when Friday comes around, she will want to do anything but see Julie in her apartment, and second, Julie will believe they are on a date which will, in turn, emphasize Cora's inability to behave like any sort of human being. Pre-emptively disembodied. And all this aside, what of her promises to Chloe? If only she had mastered the art of the No Show, the Call to Cancel, the Feigned Illness. Stuck, ineffectual Cora will be on a date with Julie next Friday night.

On the metro ride home that evening, Cora can't tell if she's more nervous about sending the postcard or venturing into the video store. Dark glasses and a deep voice had somehow become her story.

She loiters for a few minutes at the mailbox outside the grocery store. The last time she gave her friend something from great-grandmother's house, Theresa disappeared. Who knows what will happen this time? Maybe the card is a bad idea. Should she just call like a regular person? No, that would end up either disastrous or awkward. Cora didn't know which would be worse. It was just a gift, a fun little gift!

Eventually this curse will need to be broken. The postcard

will be Cora's proof that the universe can expand without catastrophe. Or at least she'll use it to test the hypothesis. Suddenly, almost on impulse, Cora drops the card in the box. No going back. No decisions, no revisions. No time to think. No time to care. No time to change the past. Focus on the future, Cora. That is all there is to do.

She turns toward the video store, a walkable distance away, but no one would judge if she drove. Just two weeks ago, renting a VHS tape was an event of little consequence. Why should the present be any different? After his rebuff, then absence, what should she care if he acknowledges her existence? Her train of thought continues its assault on the structure of the universe, the powers that be, the Lord that takes pleasure in them that fear. Fearless Cora, stepping inside a video store.

He is here. At the counter helping another customer. Cora can do this! Careful to avoid eye contact, she begins to peruse the shelves. The oversized poster for *Blow* once again offends her taste for elegant titles, except that Penelope Cruz, ominous and inviting, can't help but rescue the whole affair. But she can't think about that right now. She has a difficult decision to make. Her rental choice must be accurate, aligned with her rental history but redemptive of *Legally Blonde*, intelligent, but not snobby, cool, but not insipid.

The new release wall hardly offers anything to hold her attention. She peruses in reverse alphabetical order, as always, but can find nothing to fit the bill. *Traffic, Pollock, O Brother Where Art Thou, The Beach, All the Pretty Horses*. The scan was too quick! Too cursory to be useful. How would it look for her to return to the beginning, amble along the wall again? There must be something there that would work, but she paid so little attention. A mistake! She should have taken more time.

The one other customer in the store has left. Cora's eyes dart toward the clerk from out in her periphery. Does he know they are alone here together? His laptop computer seems to be all that holds his interest. Shouldn't he be working? She is a customer, after all, and perhaps she needs some service. He'd probably give no notice at all if she walked the length of new releases ten times over! Cora considers taking *Pollock* to the counter just to spite him. It's Ed Harris as Jackson Pollock, for god's sake. That would get his attention.

He hadn't looked up. Doesn't he understand he is now part of Cora's story? Surely this is purposeful obstinance. How could she rent a movie now, after such a refusal? There is no way to proceed with nonchalance. No. The only choice now is to leave empty handed. Maybe that would show him. She walks toward the door, thinking at least he would offer a Good Day. Nothing. Cora is a wounded animal. She slinks back to familiar surroundings, impatient for Chloe's embrace.

PART THREE

PART THREE

THE METRO WINDOW IS a moving picture full of secrets. The reel spins on despite its stops and starts. In the steady rhythm of the tracks, Cora hears the ticking whirr of a third-grade movie-day film projector almost past the credits. Each image steals a small part of a minute that she will never get back again. Junkyard cars. Dirt-crusted machinery parked haphazardly behind unkempt backs of buildings. The pretty boulevard just on the other side has no clue what's hidden here. Dumpsters and grease-spotted heavy tools, piles of lumber soaking up rainy days. Rust-colored footage dances with smoke grey thematic interludes, dusty underbellies display themselves from behind the scenes. Backlots wrestle with Cora's tea-time aesthetic, offer her repulsions to endure. All this dilapidated beauty exists as the product of Cora's imaginative labor, while Cora herself sulks in her seat like a number in the hundred-thousandths place.

Several small image-thoughts interrupt the scene: the corner of a postcard as it disappears into an unconcerned mail slot;

the calendar square marked by a postponed date with Julie; dark-rimmed glasses of a video store clerk who has rendered her inconsequential. The date with Julie had been put off, thankfully, due to an unexpected trip to Newport to visit her parents. She had asked Cora to go along, an act of flippant arrogance, or negligence, or disrespect. Cora couldn't decide which. Did she really expect Cora to leave Chloe all alone for several days to go gallivanting around Rhode Island? How could she even think to ask? Cora had plucked a socially acceptable excuse from the library bookshelf: the house cleanup deadline truly was looming and Cora truly needed to get some things done. The excuse wasn't a lie. They rarely are.

It's all getting quite rude, or at the very least disorganized. Disgruntled seems almost right. Aggrieved. Annoying. Tiresome. Vexing. Cora is having trouble finding the right word. It must be playing hide-and-seek somewhere in the poetry outside, somewhere Cora will never find it. Terrible start to the workday.

Cora rushes in to work, determined to make something of the day. Freshly poured coffee vibrating to the sound of Susan's Thursday newsprint amuses the hand that tries to hold it still. Susan's words meander in and out of understanding, none magnetic enough to stick despite Cora's dutiful bursts of eye contact. In truth, Cora isn't listening at all. She's busy streamlining the day's objectives: first, she will find a short hearing to finish by lunchtime, ideally on an unimportant topic so she feels slightly less compelled to do her best work. Then she'll take lunch, alone. That's as far as she gets when Susan asks a question Cora can't ignore without seeming ill-mannered. Has she heard of the Broadway play *Proof*? It's about a math genius who dies and also something happens with his daughter. Cora admits she has not heard of it, and generally doesn't keep up with such goings on about town. Susan wants to take her son to see the play in hopes it will kindle an interest in mathematics. Such are the dreams of a suffering mother, although to Cora's ears, the kid just seems like a nightmare.

Before Cora could catch herself, and almost cutting Susan off mid-sentence, the words 'Have you heard from Theresa' escape her mouth. How unnerving, to speak on impulse like that! Her torso slinks down into the desk chair, an evasive maneuver despite the lack of a feasible dodge, and despite the fact that she had brought the confrontation onto herself! The word 'typical' dances on the empty stage of Cora's computer screen. Susan recounts all that she knows: Theresa has taken an extended leave, no one knows why, and no one knows when she'll return. Susan relishes the unspecified air of gossip. She adds a parenthetical: all abstractors will now need to increase their workload to make up for the absence. The next issue needs to be completed by the deadline even though the team is short-handed. Cora's turn to relish. More work is always a most reliable pharmaceutical.

Amid this music to Cora's ears, her bandaged finger strikes its own desperate chords. It pulses under the protective gauze that's beginning to come loose, almost to the point of more conscious pain. Here is another plan for the day: investigate. Cora excuses herself politely and walks down the hall.

Only Cora and her reflection are in the restroom at the moment. The joy of an empty bathroom! The delicious silence! Complete freedom just on the cliff-edge of worry that at any moment the door will open to bring someone else inside. Cora looks down at her hand, then unwraps the blackened and bloodied finger to find a little hidden gift. The fingernail of her index finger lay supine on the bandage like a corpse on display, quiet and decayed and sad. The bruised fingertip, now exposed to the elements, seems vulnerable, unleveraged, tender like a baby. How does one proceed without a fingernail?

And what does one do with the nail that has fallen off so pitiably? Put it in the trash? That would be rather harsh. No need to be dismissive. She turns it over a few times to see it from every angle, then, without knowing what else to do, folds the entire bandage, fingernail and all, in layers of tissue paper from the box on the counter. She folds and folds it all into a perfect, four-cornered square. The dimensions are admirable, tight and punctuated with sharp edges. The idea is to insulate the nail until she can figure out how to manage its end-of-life care. Perhaps she could add it to the strange curation taking shape on great-grandmother's bathroom counter. That would be fitting, would it not, to come to a close on fine display with other emblems of disembodiment?

After returning to her desk, Cora puts the package in the front zipper section of her purse, applies to her finger the extra bandage she thankfully brought with her, and with a hint of queasiness, turns her mind to her work. The hearing shelf welcomes her at its side, waits to see which volume she will spend her time with today. Two out of the ten or so interest her, each lightweight enough to potentially finish before lunch. However, the rules dictate that she take only one to her desk at a time, a policy dating back to some former abstractor who hoarded all the good hearings for themselves. Her choices were both tech-related: the first on Telework, and the second on Spamming. Which to choose? Cora had a firm policy never to flip through a transcript before removing it from the shelf. She must work from the title alone so as not to cheat, to practice taking what she gets and acclimating, come what may. Telework seems a bit more straightforward, and shorter. Yes, this one will do. She flicks the book down with glad energy and turns to walk back to her desk.

Before the first step forward, Julie appears, stunningly quiet. A winning choice had been made, a triumph! And then Julie, blocking the path to Cora's desk. For a second, Cora hopes for another unexpected event to further postpone their date, but is reminded quickly that she has no such luck. Julie, smiling, bubbly, confirms the time and place: tomorrow night, six o'clock, her place. They will eat takeout, Julie's treat, then hang out and talk for the rest of the evening. Perfect, Cora hears herself say, matching Julie's smile. As Julie walks away, Cora worries. These plans will give her very little time to get to great-grandmother's, spend a few minutes with Chloe, decide what to wear, and leave again in time. All this bother, and a lonely Chloe to boot! Cora decides the date will last no more than two hours. Yes, two hours, at max. Chloe will need her, it'd be cruel to leave her for so long. Cora knows this as a fact. Another fact: Julie would never understand this as a fact. Next plan: on the metro ride home, find a brilliant excuse to leave early.

Telework is as easy as Cora thought it would be. The Subcommittee on Technology and Procurement Policy wants an increasing number of Federal employees to work from home since technology is progressing enough for such a possibility. Apparently, a worker shortage is causing all manner of inefficiencies, and telework might make the Federal government more attractive to prospective employees. Cora pauses on the word 'attractive,' imagines the government doing glamour shots for a high-end fashion magazine cover, some future administrative assistant applying for a position at the CDC by saying, 'I am attracted to the Federal government for its telework policies.' Language can be marvelous. But will she use the word 'attractive' in the abstract, even for her own amusement? These House of Representative mouths keep using the word, so she'd be within her rights. No, Cora can do better. Cora's words are laser-focused, precise, unambiguous, exact. As proof, she writes down at least a dozen more synonyms for precision. However, to her dismay, exactly zero are coming to mind for the word attractive. Impossible ratio. The missing nail must be obscuring the dictionary. If she wants this done by lunch, she had better just move along. Letters appear on the screen, tick-tick-tick, a times v plus e, despite her previous objections.

After two hours, the abstract is beautiful and compact and complete. Cora admires her work for only ten minutes, then proves her efficiency by moving on to the next hearing. None of her colleagues had taken Spamming, so she plucks it down, calls it hers and hers alone. Nestled snug at her desk, transcript in hand, the ritual perusing begins. Rows of black ink grow a shade darker, the office air thickens with the lack of white space. This one will be more complicated than she had hoped. Cora will need to think this afternoon, focus so as not to mis-represent the calculations of these senators and their guests. The task will require a hearty lunch, several cups of tea, and a quiet mind, the last of which may prove a difficult commodity to procure.

The Senate Subcommittee on Communications had spent a number of hours deciding whether email marketers should be required to offer consumers a way to remove themselves from mailing lists. An email address, for instance, at the end of every message so people could ask for their names to be omitted. Experts recount the many ways marketing emails clog up the internet and cause problems for legitimate electronic commerce. Lawmakers want the same rules that apply to direct marketing to apply to email marketing, but Cora soon discovers the myriad Federal Trade Commission regulations that make this seemingly simple goal a tangle of legal hurdles and algorithmic complexities that are beyond her analog comprehension. She rarely even uses email, although it's in vogue these days. Cora is lost in a previous millennium, a scribe scratching out words by candlelight.

Cora wrestles for an hour with FTC guidelines and Silicon Valley tech speak. Susan has gone quiet with her own work, and the office feels still and lonely. Perhaps a visit to Adam's cubicle will break up the monotony, or maybe she should just get another cup of coffee. Yet both would cause problems. Coffee would keep her up all night, and she doesn't want Adam to get any ideas. Besides, his eyebrows would distract her out of conversation. Best to leave all of that alone. She wonders how long it will take for her fingernail to grow back, wonders if it knows its alone. Her cubicle loses its perimeter by a magnitude of one as she stares at the partition separating her space from Theresa's. Words, misguided crusaders, force her to understand, spend the afternoon in a frantic escape from initial singularity.

TONIGHT CORA HAS DECIDED that it's time to do something about the doll situation in the third bedroom. While clearing out all the papers and magazines now resting somewhat haphazardly in the hallway, she had found, buried deep in the back of the closet, about twenty old dolls in various states of dress. They must be from the nineteen forties, or fifties, or maybe sixties, some wearing very few clothes, some dressed fully in their original ensembles, some in good repair, others with gouged eyes and missing hair. They lay toppled in a mishappen pile, a mangle of arms and legs and fingers and toes. They are the undead unearthed to haunt Cora, sad children with painted eyes, skin chipped as if excessive. And now Cora must determine how to handle them with minimal upset. Nothing can convince her that these creatures cannot feel. How can something with a face exist for so long and not have a soul?

This will be an event, and Cora is ready. She puts on her

most comfortable shorts and t-shirt, gives Chloe an evening snack, and even spends a few minutes playing with her so no pangs of neglect would interrupt the proceedings. Music brightens the mood and drowns out night sounds, the house's moaning and cracking and sighing. The Glenn Miller Band's greatest hits - Pennsylvania 6-5000, Moonlight Sonata, Georgia on My Mind – perfect for such an occasion. Great-grandmother must have adored Glenn Miller because about a dozen different records live in her collection. Cora couldn't blame her. The classic big band sound of brassy horns and jazzy saxophone almost makes Cora want to relive her swing dancing days, or pretend she's in a nineteen-forties melodrama, or on an ocean liner bound for the continent.

The music exists in the living room but fades toward the back of the house. As the sound diminishes, so does the mood, especially as Cora looks again on the pile of little dolls needing her attention. At first, the plan was to put them all in one large box to be appraised or donated. Surely some of these would be worth even a little money, some collector might appreciate their authenticity. Cora taped the bottom of one of the larger boxes from the kitchen and placed it next to the dolls. At this point, a number of second thoughts stumble in. Look at the smallest one in its tiny layette. Can she take the tiny thing from its friends, put it in the box, close the lid and leave it in the dark? The axiom of choice and its contradictions tell Cora It must be done, It can't be done. These sad creatures, hidden away likely for decades, thrown back into obscurity, together, but alone, just when they are allowed the chance for a breath of fresh air and a bit of sunshine? The extent of Cora's disorganization mirrors the depth of her empathy. Still, best to err on the side of caution.

Cora picks up one of the ugliest dolls. Dark, deep-set eyes, long eyelashes, cropped hair the work of a child hairdresser happy with scissors. Its cheeks and arms look bruised, dirty yellow knickers fall uneven on its legs. Cora is unsure whether to feel sorry or scared. It's heavier than she thought, and more frail.

What this doll needs is a little music. A few days of living in the outside world, some light, some air, some noise and life. If nothing else, it would ease Cora's guilt. Just for a few days, and then it will be no problem stowing it away for a new adventure. A little joy before the terror.

Carrying it like a baby in her arms, Cora brings the doll into the living room and sits it upright on the sofa just next to the record player. Glenn Miller is good company, as are all of great-grandmother's trinkets. Already the doll's face seems brighter, surprised, blushed. Cora straightens out the knickers, pats it on the head, and makes her way back to the third bedroom.

One by one, the dolls are brought out and lined up on the couch like a little chorus. The blonde beauty with flowing curly hair and a pale porcelain face. The fair brunette whose hair hides her eyes. The tallest one with red lips and eyes that seem in conversation with some ancient grown-up. The baby with the scarred face wearing a grey jumper that used to be white. A naked infant with a crocheted pink hat, lips pursed in wait for a bottle. The one with a dirty blue towel wrapped around its neck like a cape. The ragged Raggedy Ann that Cora remembers from childhood. And several less distinct ones with gnarled arms and skinned elbows and knees. They all sit facing the television set as children do, next to great-grandmother's decayed chair where Cora sits with Chloe each night before bed. All rescued, all given a second life, all now listening to music, feeling Chloe's soft fur as she curls around them to investigate.

Finally, Cora is making progress on the task she was assigned to do! The bedroom closet is almost empty of dolls and papers, and each new glimpse of carpet brings a swell of anticipation for the job ahead. After another hour, Cora notices that the darkness outside has found its way into the house, as it does. Time to take a break for the night. Only one hour until Judge Sheindlin, so she'd better feed Chloe and begin her nighttime ablutions. Cora performs her rituals slowly, making time to tend to her finger, then settles into the rickety chair with a cup of tea. She and Chloe and the dolls all together will see what's on the docket for tonight.

SHE WAKES TO CHLOE pouncing at her feet. Cora tends, in those first few minutes of the day, to twitch her toes under the covers. Chloe finds it all a splendid game. Cora does too, and feels a sleepy kind of joy, trying to put her feet under the thickest part of the blanket so Chloe's teeth can't actually break the skin. No matter if it does. She's used to it. Cora considers herself one giant cat toy, and has the scars to prove it.

Chloe quickly gets bored and jumps down to her food station, which Cora keeps by the bed so Chloe doesn't need to go out in the dark at night. In the face of the empty bowl,

Chloe's playful wake-up call quickly turns to an accusatory Get Up, Lazy! Cora eventually obliges. This, the morning dance.

Her legs slide from under the covers and remind Cora that tonight is the date with Julie. Is it a date, really? Or just a friendly get together? Cora doesn't know definitively, but can deduce from the way Julie touched her shoulder that she should probably be prepared. Panic ushers her to Chloe's food bowl and then into the kitchen to brew some coffee. What is she going to wear? After all, it's just a normal workday so would she really need to change? Maybe just keep it casual, jeans and t-shirt. But which jeans? Which t-shirt? Cora doesn't have time to answer all of these questions right now. She'll leave it to figure out during the quick turnaround from work to date. The less time to think the better. No need to accidentally drive herself crazy.

Chloe follows Cora around the house during all the morning preparations. Her spot on the bathroom rug must be full of cat hair by now, but Cora doesn't mind and rarely takes the time to clean it. Stepping out of the shower is always pleasant. She makes sure to dry her feet and shins even before her face so Chloe's affection won't leave a trail of wet fur.

On her way out the door to work, Cora remembers that her purse still cradles the carefully preserved fingernail. Strange, taking it to work for a second day. It needs to stay home. But where to leave it? She can't risk it getting lost somewhere in the house, which in fact is a feasible scenario given all the clutter. The bathroom seems the most logical place, on the counter where things rarely move around. But what about the shower condensation that would ravage the thin tissue? Cora, quick on her feet, finds some tape and zips it all around the little package, four corners in a perfect square. That should do it. No moisture can get in there. She places the bundle on the bathroom counter, promises Chloe she'll be back by five o'clock, and dashes out the door.

Cora drives to work today, wondering what topics will cross her desk and dreading the night. Her sweater wilts in the hot day, but will be needed for the chilly office. Instead of taking it off, she blasts the air conditioner, aims the vent at her flushed cheeks. Her car arrives without incident, finds a parking space, and scoots her into the workday with care.

The postcard of Chartres Cathedral begs for attention today, distracts her from the inked transcript that also demands consideration. A memory fades into view, a younger Cora sits on a church pew, silence punctured only by occasional Bible verses read in French. Words lost in the grey walls of anonymity, un-comprehended sound waves pirouetting in obscurity. Art for art. Acoustic resonance for its own sake. In that moment long ago, Cora's delirium blissfully precluded summary. No sense, no abstract. Nothing to condense. Only the music of the spheres orbiting the nave down to the last Amen.

Today, Cora wishes for the absence of language, or at least for a foreign tongue she cannot understand. Either would allow her to escape her incarceration with the Clean Air Act, over which, she is learning thanks to the Senate Committee on Environment and Public Works, there is astoundingly little oversight. She can imagine just now the tiny particulates of polluted air entering her body on the way into the video store, fusing to her lungs, passing by the counter along with her. It's a death sentence she must compress into a margin space of only three inches!

Before lunch, Adam stops by, which he does infrequently. Cora is thankful for the jailbreak. She hears him say, 'You've been avoiding me since our last lunch date.' Date? Was it a date? Is he using the term casually or does he expect something more from her? These thoughts make their way into,

'Yeah, I've been busy with extra work since Theresa left.' Excellent save. And to spare any possible feelings, adds, 'I haven't really talked to much of anyone lately.' It was all true, no one could say otherwise, not even Adam. He told her they should get together again when things slow down, and Cora agrees in spite of her true intentions. Cora always gets caught off guard. She endures more chatter about an upcoming golf tournament and some trip to upstate New York and a work project that is taking longer than expected. He asks where Theresa has gone and Cora has to say she doesn't know. Susan chimes in from her side of the wall that Theresa may or may not be returning.

He leaves, and Cora is free to return to her own thoughts. Chloe will be left alone for so long today and tonight. Maybe the dolls will keep her company. Is there any way to be excused from this silly date without suffering for it the following week at work? Plans to cancel materialize then evaporate in the space between words on the page. It's hopeless. The night will need to proceed, unimpeded. Until then, vehicle exhaust systems, childhood asthma, and particulate matter will depress the afternoon as Cora refines her techniques of avoidance.

The drive home is an oncoming tension headache. Hopefully the stomach knots go away before Cora is expected to eat the take-out meal Julie will offer her. Why and how did she get herself into this? Cora sees herself as on a movie screen, seated in the back row of a dark theatre watching the surfaces of a body drive a car along the beltway.

Chloe's faithful greeting waits at the door, deeply loving hugs, nudges from nose to cheek, a long stretchy drape over Cora's shoulder. Apologies all around. Sorry I was gone for so long. Sorry I need to be gone longer. Sorry I can't stay. I wish I could stay. Recompense comes in the form of an extra dollop of morsels and gravy. Such a quick turnaround leaves time for little else. Cora slips on a pair of blue jeans and a black t-shirt, a uniform fitting the unknown, as she wonders if the smell of great-grandmother's house has permeated the fabric. Perhaps it can garrison the perimeter, put Julie off if she tries to get close.

Cora grabs the door handle to leave the house and everything stops. She waits for the moment to pass. Something like paralysis falls over the house, nothing moves except the slow blink of Chloe's eyes. There must be a way to get out of this. She asks Chloe, 'Chloe, how can I get out of this?' But Chloe doesn't know. Just then, another panic. Shouldn't she bring something to the evening, a bottle of wine, a small bouquet of wildflowers fit for Julie's bohemian aesthetic? Isn't there a rule that one should never show up at someone's house empty handed? There's no time for an errand. This obstruction suddenly takes the shape of a brilliant idea. She will bring something from great-grandmother's house. Julie's eclectic home décor will adore it, and Cora can relax into one last hope that Julie will vanish from her storyline as well. A quick look around, and Cora sees a small crystal vase with transparent blue and orange hues colliding in the center. It has a feeble, antique spirit. Perfect. Delicate fingers trace the rim to affirm its existence. Cora picks it up, wipes it down with the softest cloth she can find, and disappears out the door.

CORA ARRIVES ON TIME even after searching for a parking spot for over twenty minutes. What a lament that she doesn't need to search for longer! She had been looking forward to a long walk to Julie's door, a ready-made excuse for being late.

Julie greets Cora wearing a tank top and cut off sweatpants. This is what she wears for a dinner guest? For someone whose

shoulder she has touched with romantic undertones? Cora
feels overdressed even in jeans and a t-shirt, but that's to be
expected. She always makes the wrong choice. What else
could she have done? Wear her own version of house clothes,
the ones she reserves for Chloe's eyes only, the ones she wore
to clean out the third bedroom? No, she had done well this
evening. There was no other choice, really, for Julie's house.
Cora breathes a little at the conclusion of this silent dialogue.

The apartment's melancholy meets Cora at the door along
with Julie. A basement with two slivers of glass that don't
even try to call themselves windows, music and children
sounding low from the house upstairs, and a punctuation mark
of incense. Probably double parentheses, over-indulgent, un-
necessary.

Tucked in the corner of the main room is an afterthought of
a kitchenette, a two-burner stovetop next to a mini-fridge and
toaster oven. Julie once told Cora she brushes her teeth in the
kitchen sink, now cluttered with dishes and a dirty sponge.
Nearby sits the food, still in Styrofoam take-out shells. A futon bed holds itself upright against the only blank wall, just
opposite a tiny TV/VCR combination. Lava lamps and dark
shades seem to make the room darker than if they were turned

off. Cora is convinced a headache will accompany her home.

Julie is entirely at ease despite Cora's presence. Annoying. Cora is pre-occupied with whether her gift, still hidden in her purse, could find a suitable place here. If not, could she leave it to languish? Considering the alternative would likely be the incinerator or a dusty thrift store shelf, Cora had little choice in the matter. The good vase would find its way into the uninformed décor, if not right away, eventually, after Julie's eclectic travels brought it a few companions. Delightfully lost in disarray, orphans, all of them, brought forth for no other reason than to ignite someone else's recollections. A gentler incineration, at least.

Within peripheral earshot, words to the tune of Julie populate the space. A timbre of monotony, a contiguous shade of green. She is saying something about a manager who is very nice but expects her to work overtime to reduce indexing backlogs. A complaint. How can she say No to the nicest man in the world? Cora doesn't know, and suddenly feels a foreboding anger at the thought of Julie failing to display her vase prominently in this cave she calls home.

Next, she talks about the food. She hopes Cora likes chicken curry. Yes, sounds delicious, although I thought you were a vegetarian? Julie recounts several stories about her stint with vegetarianism, her meat cravings, her vitamin B12 deficiency, her eventual return to existing as an omnivore. She warms their dinner in the tiny microwave, which, from a few feet away, Cora notices is filthy inside. Hopefully the edges of the plate don't touch the microwave walls! What does one do with such disgust while in someone else's house? Pretend not to care, pretend to be listening to every word Julie says, pretend to be delighted with laughter at the thought of sharing a meal in this woman's lightly contaminated apartment?

Julie's mouth never stops moving. Chewing, talking, both at the same time. Her weekend in Newport, mother's cataract surgery, father's model ship collection. She may be looking for a new job soon, indexing is too boring, she wants to change the world instead. Maybe law school if she can get motivated enough. Cora wishes she liked Julie better, or that Julie could tell a better story, or that any of it would seem to matter.

Eventually the conversation tumbles headlong into Theresa. Elation and dread fight it out in Cora's unconscious. Would she accidentally give something away, something of her obsession, of the bracelet and the brooding? Julie heard from a mutual friend that Theresa is moving to Michigan with her boyfriend. Boyfriend. Boyfriend? Like an echo, or a mantra. How could she not have known about a boyfriend? One so close that she'd move a thousand miles away to be with him? Were they even friends at all? Cora careens toward the nearest star, kicked out of orbit by a random piece of space garbage. Or she's sent back to earth a crumbling statue of David. Half thoughts. Blind nods. The evening smiles across the room from Julie but Cora has jumped timelines.

A heavy laugh leaves Cora's mouth when Julie tells her she ought to try indexing. Be careful, Cora. Inappropriate laughter will give you away! She has to decide, and quick. The decision must be based on several new pieces of information. First, she is in shock but cannot reveal it. Second, Theresa considered her less of a friend than anticipated. Third, she will likely never see or hear from Theresa again. So, what is there to do at this moment in time in a living room dirty with verbosity? Think, Cora. Keep laughing just enough, say a few words, but mostly, think.

Theresa, even mourned and beautiful, isn't everything. Julie has purpose and a kind of dignity. Susan complains and cele-brates in just the right tenor. And then there are all the others, who do well for brief moments of distraction. Theresa is a porcelain doll. You look but do not touch, a cracked face right down the middle gives her both more and less value. All in all, life is simpler without her in it, no constant draw, fewer disruptions. No one to draw her out of the process of abstraction, no audible inhalation lurking in the periphery. Theresa's departure is a triumph, if anything. Yes, a triumph! And if she's found love and happiness in the process, well, all the better. Cora can close the door, step into the alley they call liberation. Julie has saved the world after all, has given a gift, the gift of truth! And now Cora can relax into whatever the current moment brings. No more wondering, thinking, no more fear of exposure, no more postcards, no more waiting. Yes, Cora is free of it all!

Sound waves monogrammed with Cora's name reach toward her with steady hands. A voice a galaxy's distance away suddenly maps itself onto her awareness from across the little dining table. Sound and voice make words that tell Cora about Julie's admiration for the woman who runs the Thai restaurant where she picked up the food: her dirty uniform, her black shirt unbuttoned to her breast, her lipstick, the bright red stains on her teeth. Cora laughs with Julie, who with a mouthful of chicken masticates between syllables. Cora says without thinking, Yeah, there's a video store clerk I see all the time with equally memorable qualities. Less comical, more formidable, immersed in typing instead of his job, cute though, and tall. Descriptions can't stop themselves from standing stage center, the children's section, the porn room right beside it, the posters and the slow, disheveled customers rummaging through the shelves. Two sets of teeth giggle between forkfuls.

As Julie clears their plates and empty food containers, Cora decides the time is right to offer up the gift. Some kind of symbolic logic massages the moment, but Cora can't quite figure out how it operates. She wishes she had taken that one philosophy course in college but she was too intimidated by the young professor. At any rate, the vase was a good choice, not only for its more ominous associations, but also because it actually fits nicely with Julie's eclectic décor. Its cheery disposition will surely bring some light and life to the place.

The front pocket of her purse reminds her that Chloe is home alone. No time for that sadness now, though, one must keep moving! I brought you a little gift, she tells Julie, just a little something to say Thank You for dinner, and for getting her out of great-grandmother's house for an evening. She's been so busy cleaning and really hasn't gone out other than with

Julie, maybe a little unhealthy, what with so little human interaction beyond work. Cora's foibles decide to be unabashed tonight.

Cora hands over the vase and Julie seems properly pleased. She looks it over, makes a few remarks about Cora's great taste, asks where she got it. Second-hand, straight from great-grandmother's antique house of wonders. Cora said she couldn't bear to think of it in some stranger's living room, wanted it to stay in the family, so to speak, somewhere it would be appreciated. She pretends she's had a great fondness for the vase since childhood, said it had always been there, part of her life in its unassuming way. Julie changes her gaze, and suddenly Cora feels as if she has made a terrible mistake. Why such an expression of intimate deep attachment, which Julie is, as these thoughts are roaming, undoubtedly projecting onto Cora's feelings for her? Why claim it to be some heartfelt token? Such embellishment, while fun in the moment, traps Cora in whatever turn of events follows. A tragic miscalculation. All there is to do now is play the wait and see game, go along at risk of seeming rude.

Julie suggests watching a movie and, of course, Cora agrees. The TV strobes between channels as the two begin to search for something that fits the mood. A quick glance through Julie's VHS tapes indicates that she has poor taste, so Cora doesn't hope for much. The two women curl up on the futon, knees tucked under bodies in postures of ease, as if completely comfortable with the other's proximity. Julie's arm stretches out to find just the right angle to work the remote. Pale skin, light freckles. How would this arm feel to touch? Or be touched by? Pleasant? Or merely endured? Cora realizes at that moment that she hasn't touched another human being for many months. Maybe even a year. Could it be that long? Longer? Julie touched her shoulder that day, so that counts, doesn't it? Either way, tonight may rescue her from further investigation.

The television settles on some nineteen-fifties movie on AMC, but neither of the women are very interested. Julie's body inches closer as she tells a story about watching an old movie one night with her mom when they couldn't sleep. A vaguely interesting anecdote. Cora genuinely wants to hear more but before she could say so, Julie moves closer and puts her hand on Cora's. The two interlace fingers in a gesture taken as intimacy. Cora is caught. Every workday after tonight will be impacted by the choice Cora makes right now. Leave,

even after the vase and the sentimental overtones? Give in?
Just to see what it feels like?

Before she could make up her mind, Julie's lips were on her
own. A true romantic encounter is beginning and Cora is nowhere in sight. Her hands trace Julie's back, feel the weight of
Julie's hair draped over her arm, her neck accepts Julie's soft
lips, their fingers touch, breasts touch, legs and arms touch.
Warm. Not unpleasant. Julie stops to look Cora directly in the
eye. Unnerving. What does she want? Had Cora done something wrong, made some unknown inconducive gesture? The
moment endures itself a breath longer then disappears behind
the tank top Julie has just removed from her body. Behind the
black bra and behind hands that now rest between Cora's
thighs. Behind the vase that sits just beside.

Cora becomes a mirror image, two dimensions in constant
motion, one regarding the other from some distant meaning of
existence. She removes her shirt, her bra, slightly embarrassed
by its nude color instead of black, and allows her hand to rest
on Julie's breast. They recline simultaneously, without plan or
theory, and close their eyes. As she feels lips on her bare chest,
Cora wonders, almost idly, how she would abstract the sensation. Which ten words would she choose out of all the words

available to her, which would entice some researcher to want to know more? It must be accurate but engaging, brief but thorough. The words must fit as perfectly in the margins as her arms fit around Julie's lower back. She sees the right phrase just there, lurking near the perimeter of darkness, but it disappears just as Julie's fingers unclasp the button of her jeans. The abstract will need to wait. Perhaps she could compose it on the drive home, in the gleaming night, while streetlights silence the scene.

ONCE SAFELY TUCKED AWAY in her car, Cora reconciles herself to guilt: for overstating the meaning of the gift, for drifting out of body on Julie's futon bed, for excusing herself early when Julie had wanted her to stay. At the very least, Cora had come up with a good excuse – the grandparents were arriving in the morning and she needed to organize a few things before they got there. In truth, the grandparents had not mentioned a visit, although it's true they *could* arrive in the morning. Julie had offered to help, but Cora turned it down. She has a system that would be very confusing to anyone else, added to which she would be constantly tempted by Julie's elegant body. A brilliant flourish if Cora does say so herself.

Julie accepts this last grace note, so the excuse is justified after all.

The highway lanes stretch wide and solemn. Only a few more miles to Chloe. Cora wonders if the night would have taken a different turn had there been a better movie to watch, or had she admitted her aversion to curry. She wonders if the video store clerk likes curry. He doesn't seem to. No way. And she should know. By this point, Cora knows him better than he knows himself.

The thought gives her a chuckle as she reaches for the radio dial. A few skips through stations lead to The Beatles' *Love Me Do*, a song she had always felt was highly underrated, such a sad sentiment hidden underneath its pop sound and bright chords. Cora sings aloud to the harmonies and decides her video store friend would most certainly enjoy the song as much as she does. Is he there right now? Maybe she could ask him. It's a Friday night. Does he have someone in his life who would prefer him not to work on the weekends? Does he ignore them as well?

It couldn't hurt to drive by and see, sate some curiosity, draw some conclusions. And besides, the excitement is a nice distraction from the weight of Julie's soft goodbye. Will his usual uniform of laptop and button-down white shirt accompany him on a busy Friday night? Or does he change it up on the weekends? Cora will know just by walking through the door.

The car speeds a little in anticipation as another Beatles song comes on, then another and another. Could it be a station devoted solely to John and Paul and George and Ringo? Could she have truly struck radio gold? How long would it last? No one knows, but she had better appreciate it while it's here. The final few miles to the video store hear an exuberance called Cora's voice singing along to *Paperback Writer* and *Hey Jude* and *Let It Be*.

She sees him from the car, uniformed behind the counter. A number of customers dot the landscape, innocent bystanders in the Dantean labyrinth of VHS tapes and stolen glances. She will make him notice her tonight.

Fluorescent lighting wraps itself around her jeans and black t-shirt. Another clerk shelves movies on the comedy section floor while *her* clerk handles the line of customers renting their selections. What now? The Beatles distracted her from making a solid plan. Chloe must be desperate by now, and here stands Cora with no organizational schematic for getting his attention! She needs to be quick. No time to consult the thesaurus.

Find a film that will impress him in some way. That should do the trick, well enough at least. Show off her intelligence, perhaps make him feel sheepish that he hadn't known of the film. It needs to strike the right tone, coolness with a hint of condescension. The drama aisle offers nothing after two times through, the foreign film section strikes a wrong note despite some sophisticated-sounding French and Italian titles. She finds him with her eyes. He has left the counter and is helping some mom find a video for her child. He must hate that. Loud, snotty children tugging at sleeves. He would want to smash the bratty little girl at great-grandmother's house, too!

Just as Cora begins to panic, Klaus Kinski's white-suited backside saves the day. How could she have missed it? A face-out image of the steamboat, the mountain clouded in mist, the artist himself regarding it all. *Fitzcarraldo*, the perfect choice. Imagine its confidence in an alphabet with the wherewithal to place it right between *The Fisher King* and *Five Easy Pieces*! She decides, as she closes in, that her new friend must have shelved this exact film. Who else would choose, for a face-out, Herzog over Gilliam? It's all rather fortuitous. The night's previous events, now as distant as the Amazonian fog, remind her that Julie would know nothing of this movie. Yes, this one will do very well. Who else but the smartest person in the room would rent it on a Friday night?

He resumes his station at the counter before she casually makes an approach. Can I get your phone number for the account? He takes the video into his hands without looking. Without even looking! His next words are 'You have a late fee for *Legally Blonde*, rented about two weeks ago. Did you want to pay that now?' Cora stumbles. Such an unanticipated question! She should have known the past would fissure the present. How could she have missed it?

Oh, yeah, I rented that for a friend and she promised to give it back this week. Can I pay it later? Well played, Cora! You fooled him! No way will he see this encounter as anything more than it is. It means nothing for all he knows! The proof is in his final 'Okay' as he turns to process the transaction. But wait, just 'Okay'? That's all he has to offer? Maybe he knows she's lying and that's why he won't engage. But then, look, he must see that she also rents films as respectable as *Fitzcarraldo*, on a Friday night no less! She prepares for the worst and begs her cheeks not to go red.

He turns the video to scan the barcode and then takes a moment to look at the cover. Just as she had hoped, his next line of sight is directly into Cora's eyes. A brief moment, a caught eye, an accidentally batted lash. He must be asking himself questions about her, about the person who would rent such a work of genius. Cora remembers what she is wearing, glad to be hidden in a black t-shirt that also happens to accentuate her blue eyes and blond hair. The transaction is finalized with an exchange of cash, then Cora, triumphant, takes the film from his hand. She hears him say 'Enjoy', so she nods with a half-smile then escapes just in time out the door. She finds the Beatles even more pleasing as she makes the drive home.

Chloe waits at the door of great-grandmother's house, as usual, with an urgency that Cora finds both exhilarating and mournful. Impatience calls for Cora to put down the purse and video and immediately hold Chloe close, knowing also that this loving encounter will render her black t-shirt unwearable without an extra-strength lint roller. The two nuzzle together, Chloe's nose against Cora's cheek and lips and neck, after which Chloe stretches her body out over Cora's shoulder so Cora can bury her face into her belly. Sounds of sweet kisses, a purr so loud it seems to hurt, a clinging cat and a clinging Cora.

An exhaustion comes over them both, so they sit in great-grandmother's chair. Cora positions Chloe's grand body across her chest so the two are face-to-face. They sit together in the still room, an active recovery from the hours apart. Cora admits that she would have rather spent the evening here, jumping over papers and playing in boxes. Who would ever need anyone else? Chloe responds with nudge to her chin. Cora says Yes, I know I'm being overdramatic. I could just call it all off, this whole thing with Julie, with everyone. I could just call it all off. Chloe's nose touches Cora's lips. Why does she let all of this happen, these scrapes that others call connection? Chloe curls her body in toward Cora's chest, closes her eyes, chirps out a sighing purr. Cora thanks Chloe for setting it all back into perspective, for helping her establish some order.

The dolls to Cora's right seem to want to know about her evening. They sit upright, full attention, and Cora considers for a moment telling them the brief version. But all that comes out is, What a mess. What a mess, she repeats with space bars between the words. The dolls keep staring straight ahead with military precision. The meaning of life for them is Cora's compassion, and her incompetence. Tragically, now, they have become her friends.

After a few minutes, Chloe jumps down from the chair and walks to her water dish. Cora takes the opportunity to remove her uniform, and instead put on her house clothes so she can spend the rest of the evening in comfort. On the way to the bedroom, she steps over endless papers still in the hallway and approximates concern over the work left to do. She has no energy for such things tonight. Tomorrow will be different, but tonight, she needs to settle into quiet. Calm. Something like that. Perhaps in the morning she will finally clear out great-grandmother's room, see if she can make some progress. Who knows what she will find? At the very least, some quirky clothes from the sixties and seventies that may be fun to try on.

She changes her outfit in no special hurry, yet mindful that Judge Sheindlin will start soon. He abandons her over the weekend, so she is determined to enjoy their Friday night. An old ceramic tea kettle prepares a cup of tea for Cora to pour in her favorite lobster mug. She could have also chosen Daffy

Duck. Each seems as non sequitur as the other, outsiders in a crowd of conformists. Mysteries.

Maybe she'll actually watch *Fitzcarraldo* this weekend. Maybe she should, in fact. Just in case he asks her about it. She saw it such a long time ago, and has such a terrible memory for details. A sense of disaster chaperones the dance. What if he asks her a question? What if she can't find an answer? She plans to overprepare by the time he sees her again.

The cracked leather of great-grandmother's chair scratches Cora's leg while crochet stitches weather their own discomfort. Time for Judge Sheindlin. The cases are complex tonight, but the good judge sorts it all out. In the first case on the docket, a middle-aged man had borrowed a middle-aged woman's car, got tickets, and now the woman is suing. Cora watches in awe as Judge Sheindlin sees right through them, unravels the truth, exposes the pair's underlying insurance fraud. How does he do it? The word preternatural comes to mind. It's one of Cora's favorites. At the commercial break, she considers a few ways she might smuggle it into work.

PART FOUR

PART FOUR

CORA AND HER CUP of tea start their Sunday morning meditation, the two sculpted in soft lines out of Michelangelo's marble. An inert Madonna sitting with her dolls, steam from a mug and her mind the only movement, along with Chloe's steady breath. The wall clock, reverent to the occasion, has gone quiet. The chair, the room, the house. Solemn sanctuary, or mausoleum. Holy and profane, finite and infinite, a maelstrom, a moment of calm. Cora gathers her thoughts in silence, sorts them out by color and weight, hopes the process will conclude before her Earl Grey gets cold. She forgets to move her body sometimes for hours. Sitting there in the uncomfortable chair, she collects and assembles a vast taxonomy of time and place.

She would need an entire warehouse full of containers to put her thoughts in their places. She imagines bins and baskets of every shape and size, stacked up to the ceiling, each labeled by subject in thick black marker. Julie is packed away in a large box higher than Cora can reach. It lingers at the top of the pile, unsteady, ready to topple. It will crush Cora if it falls. It's packed heavy with memories of the past week: unwanted cubicle visits, touches to shoulder and hair, lunch invitations turned down, guilt, evasion. The Theresa bin is even higher, and more remote, almost unreachable. Its real estate needs are rather minimal, downsized and shoved to the back of the room.

After a few minutes the metaphor begins to bore Cora despite its utilitarian design. The thoughts won't stay where she puts them anyway, so why try? One example: as much as she wants to dismiss the grandparents' early morning phone call, there it sits, an eyesore, front and center in Cora's field of vision. Why had she answered the phone? Shouldn't she be more careful these days, especially given the Julie situation? Shouldn't she know by now that the telephone will only bring questions she doesn't want to answer? No use regretting her own actions. What's done is done. The telephone had beckoned at seven o'clock in the morning and Cora had dutifully responded.

Great-grandmother's house will be put on the market to sell in approximately one month. Can you have the house finished in the next few weeks? Have you found somewhere else to live after that? Questions. Cora had very fine, very true answers. Yes, the house is coming along very well. The third bedroom is mostly cleared, the kitchen has made good progress, and that very day she plans to clear out great-grandmother's bedroom. How much has been set aside for donation or the landfill? Will you be ready for a large dumpster to be delivered next week? Questions. Very fine answers. About half is set to be donated or sold. Two weeks should be plenty of time to ready things for the junk pile. Half? That's much too much, Cora. Great-grandmother had very little of real value. See if half more can be thrown away. Half more? Instant nausea. The incinerator has fallen into the pit of Cora's stomach.

How can they be so cruel? Don't they all have some say in the matter? The bowls and the lamps and the papers and the pictures and the dolls and all the kitchen gadgets? Even the mean little girl should at least be consulted, shouldn't she? What was Cora to do? Smash her? Kill her? Suffocate them all?

Come to think of it, where *would* they live after she and Chloe finish their work here? Where would they go? Some apartment or other? Maybe one closer to work. That would be nice. But apartments tend to be so oblivious! Generally innocuous, but completely unaware. Or suppose they had to move in with the grandparents after this. No, that wouldn't do. Unless this house is completely finished in the next three weeks, the grandparents are likely to be quite upset. The grandparents' house is definitely off the table. Besides, how will she and Chloe extricate themselves from these dusty walls and corners and all this stifling air that holds them in place? Cora's contemplation sits as still as absolute zero.

A concluding paragraph wraps itself around the margins of great-grandmother's chair. Regardless of her feelings, Cora has been given a job to do, and she needs to do it. In fact, the compressed time frame has gifted her with a ready excuse to avoid all the pesky human contact that has taken her away from the task so many times. Ancillary hours simply no longer exist. No more dates, gatherings, lunches, or dinners. No more telephone calls or requests for her attention. Only work. Boxes. Papers. Dolls. Cora's draft encyclopedia will alphabetize every last item that longs for great-grandmother's touch. Every last fork and knife, ruby ring and old receipt, every last strand of silver hair still clinging to its comb. It will take focus and fortitude, a seamless neglect of all that is outside these walls, all that is not coated with the musty remnants of great-grandmother's perfume.

Cora gives Chloe a slow blink to say I love you and tells her all about the plan for the day. The mountainous task. The reality to face in opposition to her cup of tea. The dread at opening great-grandmother's bedroom door and sorting through thousands of personalities given the names necklace and shoe and nightgown and dresser drawer. Chloe returns a slow blink, unimpressed. She barely even lifts her head.

Yes, Cora's day will be filled with decisions, with hats and gloves and sweaters and sheets and undergarments and coats and tabletop doilies and three-by-five photographs of family members she never knew. But first, the day needs a shower. Clean hair and skin. Fresh clothes, comfortable yet fitted. A long think in warm water. Coerced incipience. She beckons Chloe to follow and heads to the back of the house.

As she climbs into the shower, Cora notices that a rash on her middle stomach has spread. A slight discoloration had puzzled her over the past few days, but she attributed it to the heat outside, or to some mild irritation from her clothing. Now that red stipple covers both sides of her body, she begins to wonder what it all could mean. The hot water tapers over her skin just as mild discomfort turns to a more searing burn. Perhaps a doctor's visit is in order, but then again, such a thought may be premature. The drug store surely has some sort of cream designated for such an occurrence. Certainly a visit wouldn't hold up progress too much, and wouldn't it even be necessary to eliminate the discomfort in order to do her best work? A side thought traveled the length of Cora's bitten tongue. The drug store is very near the video store, surely a quick drive-by would only bolster her energies for the work ahead.

What she really needs is a way to track the spread of the rash, especially if any doctor might get involved at some point. Will it spread daily? And where? All the way around her middle? Up her chest, down her legs? The documentation must be unassailable. Visual. No one could argue with a visual. A photograph. Yes, two pictures a day: one in the morning and one at night. Such a diligent investigation would notice if the rash should decide to get out of hand. And what a fascinating experiment to track such a thing! This is the direction Cora will take on the issue today. Once out of the shower, she will track down the Polaroid camera she saw in the third bedroom. It didn't look too old. Maybe it still works. She searches her memory for any new batteries she might have seen lounging about the house but has difficulty imagining anything associated with the word 'new.'

The camera perches itself on the far shelf in the third bedroom. Cora hadn't yet cleaned that part of the room but at least a path had been cleared to reach it. Someone must have gifted the thing to great-grandmother in the last ten or twenty years. Cora presses the red button and hears the machine whirr to life. The first picture it takes is a sideways angle of the bedroom wall. Just a test, but it works! With only three pieces of film left in the device, she had better be choosy. Three things seem worthy: her rash, the dolls, and Chloe. She points the camera at her belly and snaps a photo, then makes her way into the living room. The still-strewn papers greet her as she travels the length of the hallway. These will need to be rearranged at some point. Perhaps she could stack them neatly back in the third bedroom until she can decide what to do with them. So many decisions. The grandparents had said to cut Keep and Donate down by half. Cora dared not tell the papers or the three drying Polaroids that now join them.

———————

GREAT-GRANDMOTHER'S BEDROOM SMELLS worse than before. Damp decay, airless, still. The closed door has not been kind to the room, nor have the locked windows or the muggy August day. Cora tries to remind herself to open them tonight when it's cooler outside. If they will even open, that is. How many years has it been since the room had any contact with the outside world?

After considering her options—the dresser, the nightstand, under the bed, the vanity—Cora decides to start the process with a challenge. How prudent she is to start with the most difficult of all the tasks! The closet, bulging with clothing, bags, shoes and who knows what else would show the most progress when completed. The clothes should be easy to sort, and the shoes all very likely must be discarded without question. Yet still, there is so much of it all. And all of it so very intimate, so close to the body that once filled them, the visual expression of her movements, her gestures and sweat and skin. The closet is full of great-grandmother, whom Cora must reduce by half and then half again.

The day feels itchy like Cora's center, reddened, thick, burdened. She lifts her shirt to look at the rash, now brighter, more tender, irritated at the thought of the task ahead. It dawns on Cora, almost like the quiet itself had come to life, that she had forgotten to put on the requisite mood music. No wonder the job seems so awkward to start! A quickened pace down the hallway leads her to the old album collection where she immediately chooses Patsy Cline. Sad country wails, childhood memories of Easter visits and summer vacations. Cora decides to push through the passage of time. These songs will be a perfect mechanism to help steel herself against nostalgia.

Before she touches a single item in great-grandmother's room, Cora first indulges in some phrase work. She chooses a mantra: any organizational project begins with categorization. The sentence jumps out from the bedroom corner and takes Cora by surprise. Its presence puts a spring in her step as she carries out its declaration. One by one, she removes the clothing from great-grandmother's closet and arranges it on the bed. Shirts, still on hangers, go in the upper left-hand corner. Skirts in the upper right. Pants on the left edge and dresses all along the bottom. Jackets lay across the vanity chair, too heavy for its wobbly legs but the decision has been made. Colors fill the room like an eclectic dream, impressing each other with their showmanship. Dozens of shoes join the menagerie, each with its pair at the foot of the bed. Decades of fashion piled neatly by type, preserved in the beleaguered air.

Thirty minutes later Cora reaches the back of the closet. Empty of clothes, the space opens like a gasping mouth, almost breathless but still alive. Only a few items remain: some pictures, framed, with their backs against the wall. Everyone has a few old pictures packed away, don't they? Relics of ancient décor. Memories rendered irrelevant. What could great-grandmother have stored away here?

The first is rather unsurprising. A woman in a salmon-colored formal dress, in nineteen-forties aesthetic, stands before a doorway with her hand to her chest. She looks up dreamily, as if at the conclusion of a date that left her mind swimming. Cora carries the print into the light of the bedroom. As she props it against the wall, a detail intrigues the overtones of jilted love coming from the record player. Two of the woman's fingers slip just under the frilled edge of her dress, as if seducing the bare skin inching toward her breast. Cora backspaces her initial response and re-writes the line. Surprise is called for after all.

After unearthing the next two women, Cora notices a theme. Cora hates the word, though. Not a theme. A pattern. A motif.

Trapped in matching silver twelve-by-sixteens are two vintage semi-nudes staring intently at Cora's open eyes. Smaller in size than the salmon-dressed woman, but not in magnitude. One woman sits, painted on a thin black stool in her short nightgown, a garter belt snuggled close to her thigh. Cora has caught her removing her stockings, one shoe still on her foot, the other thrown haphazard to the side. Her nightgown has come loose, has fallen down past her breasts as she bends down to look at her own hands in the act of disrobing. The other woman, clearly imagined by the same artist, but brunette this time instead of blonde, sits and looks out directly at Cora, nightgown hiked, garter belt high on her thigh and breasts in causal view, while she picks a bright yellow flower out of a vase just to her left. She smiles in a shy kind of way. Cora smiles back from the outer edge of a blush. After a few moments of admiration, she files the women under erotic in the dictionary and puts them delicately to the side.

In total, great-grandmother had stored away twenty-four women in various stages of undress. All vintage, sleek, demure, coy, pale. Cora brings them, one by one, out of hiding, faces them out against the bedroom wall in a long, erotic single-file. The woman with her bare back to us, sitting so the top of her bottom features center stage in the painting. Two muscular women posing as nude Greek goddesses, winged, floating in a wild embrace. One stands naked in a field with a gnarled cityscape in the background. An entire bacchanal with nine women bathing each other in a lagoon, others streaming flowers around supine bodies, several touching their own breasts, wry smiles all around.

So many questions. How long had they been in the house? In the closet? Did they belong to great-grandmother? Or had she hidden them for someone else? Had she purchased them surreptitiously, then hid them from embarrassment or shame? Were they hated relics of long dead great-grandfather's proclivities? What would the grandparents say if they knew? Cora re-visions the past, Easter dinners with the women as guests, on display in the living room in place of the black-and-white family portraits. What a scandal! Great-grandmother must have had little choice in the matter, though Cora at least would have enjoyed that holiday gathering. Yes, in Cora's mind now and no matter what truth she learns in the future, these lovely ladies are the secret bounty of great-grandmother's plundered sexuality, kept out of sight, isosceles in a sea of equilaterals.

The fantasy ushers Cora into the realm of possibility. Those empty spaces above the sofa, the hollow outlines once filled with pictures of faces and old bodies. They all look out into the living room with unblinking eyes, like zeros that long to be infinity. Cora knows what she needs to do. All she needs now is a hammer and some nails. A quick search through the tiny hall closet does the trick. No more shame for these women. They, like the dolls, may have only a few more weeks to exist, so why not spend the time where they belong, hanging on a wall, masterfully placed to fill a void? Cora will cherish them enough for all of history.

Cora turns to share the epiphany with Chloe and realizes her friend is not there. Nowhere in the room, in fact. This is odd. Chloe rarely spends time in a different room than Cora. Maybe Chloe simply doesn't enjoy the ambiance of great-grand-mother's bedroom, which Cora must admit, is a little creepy. More so with all these women staring her down. But where could she be? Cora makes her way to the front of the house, thinking of the many tasks she could accomplish there. Turn the record. Survey dimensions. Check on the dolls.

Sure enough, Chloe is exactly where Cora had left her earlier this morning. In fact, she hadn't moved from the spot all day, not even to join Cora in the bathroom for a post-shower pet. Concern changes the room to a paler shade of grey. Cora rushes to check on her, gauge her mood and overall brightness. After some questions and affection, some caresses and nose-to-noses, all seems perfectly fine. Chloe purrs, enjoys the attention, even jumps down from the sofa to get a drink of water. Best to keep an eye on her, even so. Chloe curls up in the forefront of Cora's mind, first case on the docket.

Cora spends the rest of the day hanging pictures and the evening admiring her work. The ritual, full circle. All fourteen images totaling twenty-four women in perfect precision above the sofa. Not an empty face in sight. Look how the population grows! These are times that call for the haughtiness of an exponent. Not to mention the precarious existence of superscript, perched high on its invisible pedestal but shrunken down to size.

THE NEXT MORNING CORA wakes to a subsequent oddity. Chloe is missing from the bed. Where are her begging protocols? Her vicious but playful attacks? The folded blanket, or in other words, Chloe's side of the bed, is empty. She is nowhere around the room. Worry compels Cora to forego her usual early morning ruminations.

Cora finds Chloe curled up on the sofa next to the dolls, in much the same position as most of yesterday. No doubt can be had now, Chloe is definitely feeling unwell. Cora tries to get Chloe to move from the spot, to play with a toy, to push through the obvious fatigue. No luck. Gently, Cora lowers Chloe's body down from the couch to see if she can walk. She can, but the only place she travels is right back up onto the sofa to lay down. Almost twenty-four hours of enervation. How could Cora have gone to bed with Chloe clearly in such a state?

No need to panic. Just do the sensible thing and call the vet to make an appointment. Yes, Cora, stay calm and pick up the telephone. Thankfully, the practice can see Chloe at ten-thirty for an acute visit. That's only a few hours from now. Surely, she will be fine until then. She seems alert enough, can jump and purr. Yes, she will be okay until then. The next phone call informs Susan that Chloe is ill and Cora will be out for the day.

Disaster rages in apocalyptic tones within the liquid volume of Cora's morning coffee. What if something about the dolls is making Chloe sick? What if that's why they were hidden away to begin with and Cora should have left well enough alone? What if decades worth of carpet dust is finally getting to Chloe whose nose is so close to the ground? Or there is always the unthinkable, that Chloe is seriously ill, something with her kidneys that will cascade system-wide failures throughout her unprepared body. No, Cora refuses to accept the possibility, refuses to give it even a single jewel of energy. It must be environmental. Cora is determined to solve the mystery. Morning activities include investigating each room for pollutants, scouring the carpet for unusual scents, verifying the consistency of fecal matter in the litter box, and sitting next to Chloe on the sofa, stroking her back to tuneful murmurs of affection.

The time finally arrives to leave, so Cora scoots Chloe gently into her carrier. Slow and steady, she drives to the veterinary office so as not to unnecessarily jostle her friend. Chloe goes along in near silence, not a meow or chirp to be heard. At the office, Cora assures Chloe that everything will be okay, that the strange noises and sounds won't cause her any harm. Chloe's wide eyes command the fatigue to step aside. The vet examines her, checks her temperature and vitals. All normal. Ultrasound, normal. Results of the blood test will arrive later in the day. All the vet can see is a bit of dehydration. Has there been a recent change in her drinking habits? Does she tend to favor wet or dry food? No, nothing different that Cora can think of. Drinking seems normal but perhaps Cora should keep a more attuned eye. She does enjoy her morsels and gravy. Should she eat more wet and less dry? Should Cora change the daily ratio of one to the other? The prescription diet for urinary tract sensitivities is quite expensive so Cora tends to give her more dry than wet. Could that be the problem? What could be the problem, doctor? Tell Cora and she will do everything she can do to fix it. The vet suggests placing multiple water dishes around the house for easy accessibility. That, Cora can do.

They give Chloe subcutaneous fluids and send the two home to await a telephone call later in the afternoon. The day will be long for Cora. Cora does not enjoy waiting, especially when Chloe's health is involved. Something must be done with the day, but outwitting her impatience might give any task a run for its money.

Soon after their return, to Cora's relief, Chloe begins to seem more herself. The first indication: Chloe's ravenous attack on a bit of string hanging from great-grandmother's couch. The second: a hearty purr. Chloe is feeling better. Cora can feel it. But still, the telephone awaits the afternoon.

First things first. Water. Water needs to be positioned all over the house. Wherever Chloe might roam in the rooms and hallway, she will find water somewhere nearby. A quick perusal of the environment leads Cora to choose a number of advantageous spots. Definitely both sides of the living room, a few down the hallway, one on the dining room table where Chloe tends to lounge, one in the kitchen, one or two in each bedroom, one near the slant of light where Chloe soaks in the sun through slits in the dingy blinds. As Cora looks around, the place seems cozier than usual. Perhaps she could even imagine staying here indefinitely if the possibility arises, especially now that those terrible empty spots on the living room wall are filled with points of interest.

No use dwelling. A job needs to get done and Cora has a plan to do it. And what a perfect opportunity to clear out great-grandmother's kitchen cupboards! Before opening a single door, Cora already begins to imagine shelves stacked with all manner of water dishes for Chloe. Wide-rimmed cups, bowls of all sizes, coffee mugs, except the few that Cora uses, all pulled from behind closed doors. Thoroughly washed, inspected for cracks and then dried with dishtowels, the motley group is scattered all throughout the house. Three dotted between unwieldy stacks of paper in the hall, four stationed in corners of the living room, two in each bedroom, and three in the kitchen and dining area. Chloe is covered, without a doubt. Perhaps even excessively, but better safe than sorry.

The next puzzle to be solved: how will all of these bowls stay reasonably full of fresh, clean water? Dust circulates everywhere in great-grandmother's house no matter how often Cora attempts to wipe down surfaces. A system is certainly needed to keep up with such a task. Perhaps even a table drawn up with a rotating schedule throughout each week. A spreadsheet! Half of the bowls will be refilled each day, the other half the next. A simple, brilliant formula — half and half to make a whole. She could even begin to remove some of the dishes once Chloe regains full health. An excellent plan. Cora is feeling better about the state of affairs by the minute, and almost skips down the hallway as the sight of Chloe sniffing at a few of the dishes.

The kitchen cupboards must be practically empty by now.

What progress! However, Cora opens the doors to a minor disappointment. So many dishes left to pack. Where did they all come from? Is there some kind of replicator buried in the dark back corner that spits out duplicates each time one is removed? Cora is in no mood to dwell on such hypotheticals. No worry. It's nothing that can't be overcome in the course of a full day off from abstracting. Besides, a task of such magnitude will sufficiently distract her from the torture of waiting, and from the discomfort at knowing her colleagues will be examining transcripts meant for her turns of phrase. This month's issue will suffer from her absence. Such a pitiful glance back at the equal sign.

The answering machine blinks from across the kitchen, mocking Cora's aimlessness with its clear sense of purpose. Maybe it's some telemarketer selling great-grandmother a new life insurance policy or an all-expenses-paid trip to Maui. It couldn't be the vet's office since the phone hadn't sounded once since getting home. Haphazard curiosity leads Cora to push the button and listen to the voice on the other side. Julie. Of course. Of course the voice is Julie's. Of course she would call to check in, notice Cora's absence and want to know the cause. How intrusive! She asks, Is there anything I can do? Is anything the matter? She misses Cora, apparently, though the sentiment seems dubious at best. Can she bring Cora some chicken soup? Cora can think of nothing she wants less than a visit from Julie to great-grandmother's house.

The voice dies away just at the moment Cora's disappointment scurries to life. What could be the source of such an odd response? Of course. Theresa, who hadn't even spared a moment to pick up the telephone. Annoying. Not even a single message or note that she had made plans to move to another state with someone else, quit her station on the other side of the grey cubicle wall to make her way into a world that lacks Cora. It's more than annoying but the right word gets lost on the way into Cora's unconscious. Well if that's the kind of friend she is, the void can have her.

Back to the distraction. It's time. And besides, Chloe seems much better now. She's on the dining room table drinking from the newly designated water bowl. Maybe everything will be okay after all. She'd get the house done in time. She'd extricate herself from Julie. She'd forget about Theresa. The rash would go away at some point. And the video store guy would eventually realize her significance. A swelling ecstasy fills the open kitchen cupboard as Cora reaches for the first item on her to-do list.

A few dishes in, the optimism wanes. A peek into the near future unveils piles and piles of dishes chaotic on the kitchen counter, no form or rhyme, no margins to hold them in place. Cora needs a structure, a system, an organizing principle. Something at least as effective as the one she used in the third bedroom. Arrange first, pack later. That has been the internal structure along the way and it had served her well. Classify, sort, define. Then document. Codify to permanence. It's the only reasonable way. Complexity can't outwit her as long as she follows the rules.

The rules, just at the edge of great-grandmother's randomized collection of kitchen paraphernalia. Do all these dishes follow them too? Have they been, all along, a split atom waiting for Cora's hands to cool the reaction? In terms more fit for abstraction, are there matching sets scattered amid the disorder? It's a good question to answer on a Monday. In an instant, an organizational pattern dances its way into Cora's preparations. First, sort each dish into piles alongside its matches and count to see if there are full sets, four or eight or sixteen. Next, allow the data to inform her decisions regarding discard or do-nation. Another brilliant plan! It's positively mathematical! As long as she remembers to include Chloe's water dishes, nothing can go wrong.

Eight deep brown speckled plates and bowls become the first to collect themselves together. Sixteen white plates lined with pink flowers join the congregation. A set of six similarly shaped bowls fit together, although in all different colors. Eight pale white coffee mugs, four deep blue cereal bowls, three sets of four tumblers join the crew in a variety of depths and hues. Eventually it becomes clear that the white plates have lost three of the matching soup bowls, and the cereal bowls have no plates to speak of. A group of four thick dinner plates find each other in the confusion and seem thankful for it. Diasporic is the melody that sings above the fugue.

Soon the counters are crowded so once again the living room floor takes over. Her organization is impeccable. A faultless methodology. Each group reunited, singletons and odd numbers to the side, a family of misfits, as happens. No doubt the decisions would fly from Cora's mind with the con-fidence of a well-populated spreadsheet!

At the height of triumph, Cora's middle begins to remind her of its own concerns. Her rash feels worse, woolen under her shirt and radiating with what feels like bright heat. Cora lifts her shirt slightly to take a look. As expected, no victory is without its spoil. Her stomach is now screaming red and will no longer be ignored.

Cora looks at Chloe with a slow blink. Would she be okay if Cora leaves to search for a remedy? Chloe gives a slow blink in return. Yes, she says, I'll be okay. To drive the point home, she jumps down from the dining table and sniffs around at the newly formed array on the living room floor. Cora says aloud to Chloe, Yes, I know how it looks. But really, it's only a mess on the surface. Not that Chloe asks her to justify her choices. But still, it seems rude to just say nothing despite the appearance of a huge pile of dishes just where Chloe enjoys a good stretch in the afternoons.

Maybe Cora should simply go stand in the shower. After all, her medical philosophy has always held that nearly all discomfort can be alleviated, at least temporarily, by a long soak in water. She could also decide to be reasonable. The drug store would inevitably help her find some kind of medicinal cream designed for this kind of ailment. Chloe, will you be okay, are you sure? I'll be gone just a few minutes. Chloe jumps as if weightless onto the dining chair. Definitely feeling better. But still, the vet hasn't called. How long can a routine blood test possibly take? If nothing else, Cora can pick up a new toy for Chloe at the drug store. And maybe a package of Polaroid film to keep more careful track of this rash.

THE NEAREST DRUG STORE happens to be in the same strip mall as the video store. Cora doesn't plan it that way. In fact, her wish is to drive entirely in the opposite direction, to avoid temptation, to really show him the depths of her self-control. What would he think of her then? How his estimation will grow, his curiosity piqued! But there is no time to think about all of this today. Chloe is ill and Cora is in the middle of some excellent progress at the house.

Despite best intentions toward timeliness, the search for rash cream takes well over fifteen minutes. The ingredient list is the same on at least a dozen packages, the symptoms it treats, the promise of extra strength. How to choose? Eventually Cora takes one off the shelf without thinking and puts it in the basket. A whim, which is equal to fate, which is equal to choice, which is almost always equal to regret.

Polaroid film and a new toy for Chloe take much less time to find despite the obvious complications. Cat toys must be unassailable, no parts Chloe could chew off and swallow, no feathers or anything else she'd want to ingest. A long grey felt tassel on a solid plastic stick: perfect. She will love it, the two will invent endless new games to play at home.

Another decision awaits Cora in the car. It's hot so she finds The Beatles channel and blasts the air conditioner. Drive back to great-grandmothers, or a quick peek in the video store? Can the rash stay quiet enough for a perfunctory stroll just to assess the situation? Is he even working today? Maybe he only works in the evenings. Suddenly Cora feels she has been sitting in the car for an overly cautious length of time. What if he were to casually walk by on a break and see her? And what if, in that scenario, he is walking with someone else? And once again, the 'should' or 'shouldn't' carries Cora away atop the chorus of Penny Lane.

Oh! Darling's exquisite guttural intoxicates her into one last overview of pros and cons. Good thing, too, because she's forgotten a crucial element! *Fitzcarraldo* is still resting on top of the television set waiting to be watched. A near disaster. What if he remembers, asks questions? He'd ask, she'd have no response and so would fumble for something to say and seem foolish. Stupid, even. The look he had given her during the transaction indicated he's seen the film, probably even knows it by heart. No, the cons have it. Home it is, to Chloe.

But be reasonable, Cora, at the very least. Allow the song's reassurances to skirt you back to the crux of the matter. Would he really remember her specifically anyway? He must rent to hundreds of people a day. Why should he recall one customer on one night renting one single movie, even if he does know it backwards and forwards? Of course, if he doesn't remember, that only speaks poorly of him. Who could forget the one customer renting *Fitzcarraldo*? People don't exactly line up for that one. If he's worth anything, that moment alone would have been the 'event' of his evening. But maybe that's putting too much stock in her own narrative. Maybe his story is still Cora-less, even after all this time. No way to know for sure. Yes, exactly. No way to know! It's mere speculation, could go either way. Why should it keep her from a casual wander through rows of movies? Maybe she just wants to look at the titles. It's not uncommon. People do browse for the fun of it, and even rent without having seen the ones they've already brought home. People do it all the time! It's not out of the ordinary at all. A plan takes shape while McCartney affirms his own melancholy. She will go into the store, browse the shelves, and leave without renting a single video, all without even mentioning the one collecting dust by now in great-grandmother's living room.

The car makes its way to the other side of the lot and feels the presence of his white button down even before pulling into the spot. He is there. Of course. Cora walks inside the door with abandon, as if she has every right to do such a thing. His dark-rimmed glasses are the air she breathes even though she passes by without looking. A laptop separates them from each other, builds a wall between the drama section and his forearms rested on the reddish countertop. Will he look at her? Cora must find a way to be seen. He'll be thankful. Nothing on the screen can be half as interesting as an abstractor with a sick cat and a rash on her belly.

The thought ushers Chloe into the scene. At home alone after a trip to the vet. What is Cora doing? She'll be okay. Just a few minutes more. She's probably asleep anyway, likely snoozing comfortably the same way she'd be if Cora were right there. The only question is whether the blood test results have come through and irresponsible Cora is missing the call. Cora puts these thoughts to the side for just a few minutes while she walks with purpose through the aisles. Documentaries. Comedies. New releases. Always the same. How long is a film considered a new release these days? It seems like years. Proof: the ugly yellow *Bottle Shock* cover has haunted her for at least that long. Alan Rickman can't even save the design, which is too like the one for *Bottle Rocket*. Irritating. Cora often daydreams about secretly taking it off the new release wall and slipping it in some random place in the comedy section between two indistinct movies. Put it in its rightful place as one of hundreds. But she'll never actually do it. Cora follows the rules, especially when the alphabet is at stake.

On the way to the center aisle, she passes the foreign film section and sees *Women on the Verge of a Nervous Breakdown*. Intriguing. She looks but doesn't touch. Vows to rent it someday. An idea assaults Cora's delight at the very moment her eyes land on *Rosencrantz and Guildenstern Are Dead*. She will speak to him. It will happen just a few minutes from now. But what will she say? It can't be a question about a film she'd then be obliged to rent. That would imbalance the equation, and she needs each side to be equal. It can't be about a movie at all, in fact. How mundane, to talk about movies in a video store! Maybe something personal, something about the work on his computer, which, all in all, he must want to be asked about considering the prominence of the device in the mise en scène. It's a risk, but the only way to keep Klaus Kinski from joining the conversation.

Cora approaches the counter on a mission and places her hands firm on the hard surface. He looks up at her. He looks up! Can I help you with anything? A thousand responses come to mind. Keep it simple, Cora. No need to overcomplicate. Yes, actually. I hope you don't find the question disagreeable or too personal, but can I ask what you're working on there? Are you some kind of international spy under cover in a video store? Or do you own a used car business on the side? Cora's charm wraps itself around his smile.

His response: Ah, this? Well, in fact I'm working on a novel, editing it for publication. It's written, done, and now I'm just editing. Why do you ask? His question has the lyricism of a statement. No reason. Just unabashed curiosity, nothing more. Thank you for telling me. It's very cool, working on a novel in a video store. You're practically living the dream. Laugh. Laugh in response. She notices for the first time that he smiles with his eyes. Then, out of nowhere, he asks: Are you enjoying *Fitzcarraldo*? Cora's annoyance retires to the back room. Atoms collide. Her heartbeat reddens her face. She stumbles: Oh, I haven't watched it yet. Maybe this evening. Or this afternoon. So much going on. And actually, I need to get going. Cora deals him cards the color of half lies and wonders why as the door closes behind her.

THE DRIVE BACK TO great-grandmother's house is an impressionist landscape, blurred and full of light. Every song on the radio is titled Exaltation. A novel. Of course! What else could it be? But what kind of novel? Why hadn't she asked? Something beautiful and literary, surely, given his deep voice and height. It all makes sense. He writes stories; she, abstracts. He embellishes the world; she cuts it down to size. He expands; she contracts. He creates; she destroys. Such perfect balance, and he doesn't even know! The car almost turns around on its own. More questions. What has he created, exactly? And how long has it taken? And how many others has he written? And where will all of it end? Wonder. Rapture. Absolute devotion.

Chloe is in position awaiting her return. Guilt overtakes Cora's good mood. Nuzzles, hugs, a groaning purr. I'm sorry I was gone so long. But look, I got you a new toy. They start to play, Cora twisting the cattail back and forth while Chloe jumps and rolls after it. As always, the game devolves into Chloe attacking Cora's hand. She knows who's pulling the strings. Cora's joy calculates Chloe's energy level after a day of dehydration.

The answering machine blinks in the periphery. Cora hops to listen, dismayed when the voice rings out as Julie's. Again! She hasn't heard back from Cora and is worried. Please call her back to let her know all is well. All is well? Who says that? Such a pathetic attempt at syncopation! An interruption beyond the pale. Cora will not return Julie's call. No way. Although if she doesn't, she will have some explaining to do the next day at work. Maybe she should call just to avoid a later confrontation. Or even worse, the possibility of a surprise visit. The horror! Yes, get it over with, then spend the rest of the evening with Chloe, and maybe *Fitzcarraldo*.

Julie's answering machine picks up. The universe has come through after all. A short message, very little detail. We are

fine, all is well. Chloe's under the weather so we stayed together today. Took her to the vet, waiting on results. Hopefully I'll be at work tomorrow. See you then. All truth. All lies.
Cora's theory of relativity.

The annoyance summarized according to scale, Cora now
turns to the order of the hour. The rash. She lifts her shirt once
again to take a peek. Yes, it's grown. Certainly. Or at least it's
become more intense. Does that count as growth? Puzzling.
Cora revisits the trajectory of the last few days. Has she
touched anything out of the ordinary? Contracted a virus
somewhere along the way? Maybe it's the escalator handrails!
No telling what manner of microscopy attached itself to Cora.
Then why on her stomach? Maybe it's simply the gods smit-
ing her for the encounter with Julie. A cosmic warning not to
step out of bounds. Yes, that makes much more sense.

The unwavering Polaroid set to work on its documentary
project. The rash, a little shy, projects itself only with doubt.
Cora must coax it out of hiding. Reveal its subtleties. Or the
very least, affirm the unreliability of her own imagination. She
maneuvers the camera to take another photo and then places it
alongside the one from earlier. Interminable wait. She watches
as the light takes the shape of her waistline. Sure enough, a

few more spots have appeared since this morning, mostly on the right side of her stomach. Another awkward pose offers a view of her back, proving without a doubt that Cora is now encircled by whatever has decided to join her on the journey of life. Avoid scratching, she's been told, though most of it was itchy to the point of burning. The new cream should help, but Cora hesitates. Is it the correct remedy? What if this specific type of cortisone only makes the rash angrier? What then? Maybe she'll just wait until nighttime and see if it all goes away.

Now what to do with these photographs. Cora admits they do look strange, blotchy and pale, old freckles out from hiding, her skin like the texture of leather left too long in the sun. So many people have seen this patch of skin over the years. Cora feels sorry for them, thankful they hadn't turned away in disgust.

The pictures need to stay in chronological order for scientific purposes so she writes numbers in a large font across the back. Meticulous notation. Yet still, there must be a more visual form of data analysis available. Like a collage. Or the many-stringed wall of an amateur sleuth hunting down the whereabouts of a serial killer. Something along those lines.

For example, hang them in order on the wall near the bathroom mirror. Perfect. She can add one each morning and evening to track the expansion with little trouble at all. Excellent solution! Despite the unpleasant nature of the images, the plan seems ideal. Except, that is, for the shower steam issue. No matter. She's already worked that one out. Great-grandmother has an entire box of sandwich bags lying in wait for just such a scenario. Place each photo in a bag, zip it up, then hang it on the wall. She begins the process in one long column all along the side of the mirror, figuring she must have *some* rights to the bathroom wall after all this time. And in fact, though individually quite ugly, when put altogether the pictures exhibit an oddly artistic sensibility, almost museum quality, if Cora does say so herself.

Cora notices the time just as the clock turns to four o'clock. The vet's office closes in just one hour. Thirty more minutes. That's all she will give them, then she'll call. No one wants to be a nuisance, but she needs to know. Depending on the results, her evening will be spent in worry or relief. Or guilt. She did stay gone all day and all night for the date with Julie. But that was a week ago now so this couldn't possibly be related. Could it? And isn't it strange that she and Chloe both got sick together. She with her rash, Chloe with her thirst. It strikes Cora that the rash might after all be related to the mole that had fallen from her stomach only a few weeks ago. Such a thing as that shouldn't really be free of consequence.

Just as this line of questioning begins to take a sour turn, the phone rings out louder than usual. It must be the vet. What if it's Julie? Or the grandparents? Answering the phone has never been accompanied by this much danger. Odds are, it's the vet. The timing is just too suspicious. For Chloe's sake, she needs to answer. At the risk of disaster, a ruined week, a haphazard acquiescence. For Chloe, she would brave all manner of perils.

It's the vet. Cora is granted a reprieve after all. Chloe's blood work looks just fine, very good for a cat her age, in fact. Just leave a few extra water bowls around to encourage her to drink. Cora turns on the charm. I'm way ahead of you, doc.

As soon as she hangs up the phone, Cora's stoicism gives way to tearful convulsion. A heaving fit of crying guides her toward Chloe's soft body. Chloe, you're never allowed to be sick again. Cora is playing and not playing. She picks Chloe up and holds her for a moment, cheek to cheek the two sway to silent music, sway to the sound of Cora's weeping and

Chloe's circulating blood. Soon Cora's face is simply too wet to continue. Chloe jumps to the ground and Cora makes her way to the bathroom to find some tissues. She looks in the mirror. Face red and glistening, cat hair on her lips and black t-shirt, scratches on her arm from when she played as Chloe's prey. This woman in the mirror is the human being Chloe has decided is hers. Cora cannot stop from crying.

Chloe follows her into the bathroom and wants to be pet. Cora picks her up, looks at the pair of them reflected in the glass. Cat and girl, each as significant as the other. Almost lookalikes. The journey they have found is toward each other, toward treats and worry and nestling on the pillow, toward warmth and noses touched to noses. Chloe nuzzles to Cora's wet cheek, uses her paw to clean herself with the damp of Cora's tears. Only the mirror is witness to such love.

Chloe gives Cora's forehead a cursory lick before jumping down to the counter with little hesitation. The loving is over for the moment. Cora quiets her crying and watches as Chloe nudges items leftover from great-grandmother's ablutions. She paws at Cora's cup, so it gets moved to the other side of the counter, just under the collage of photos. Artifacts line the space, mole and nail and rash, the bodily remnants of Cora's failing psyche. A triptych of holy relics from ancient times on crude display in a dead woman's home.

Cora pulls herself out of her melodramatic ruminations and follows Chloe into the hall. Scattered papers whisper in the grandparents' voices. Four more weeks. Only four more weeks. From out in the living room, dinner sets taunt her with a lack of symmetry, their isolated patterns strewn wide in only a semblance of order. If the grandparents were to arrive right now, they would have no idea how close she is to finishing. Her methods would be lost on them, as would her ability to bring what is hidden into the light.

Cora sits on one of the sparkled yellow dining chairs where she can see the kitchen and the living room all at once. Chloe's gaping yawn greets her from the sofa. Let's do an inventory, shall we Chloe? There's not really that much left to do. Wrap and box the dishes, pick up papers and somehow throw most of them away, finish the third bedroom and great-grand-mother's bedroom and the bedroom they have slept in for al-most a year. Box up dolls, take down nudes, throw away most of the kitchen. Cora's fatigue meets the sneering face of the little girl who also must be boxed and shipped away. At least she can take her raggedy doll with her, though he still looks up at her in terror. What must she think of these bare-breasted women who wink at her from across the room? Cora decides the pictures will be the last thing to go. Hopefully she'll have the courage to make the little girl the first.

PART FIVE

PART FIVE

THE CURTAIN RISES AND Cora sits serenely at her desk, typing. Susan's rustling papers can be heard faintly over the quick tick-tick-tick of keystrokes. A bright morning sun pierces the window to Cora's right, yellowing her face against a backdrop of corporate grey. Thin-framed eyeglasses house a tiny reflection of blue light from the computer screen, the cursor dancing in microscopic flecks next to her pupils. She sits very still in a black chair. Off-stage, anonymous co-workers populate the soundscape with coughing and quiet chatter.

Aside from the words per minute promenading across the page, Cora's cube-shaped bubble is vacuum sealed in stillness. Desk papers dare not move an inch, pencils and pens stand at firm salute in an old plastic cup, manila folders have lined up their tabs, and even the wheels of her chair have locked themselves tight in fear of some sudden shifting weight. In short, the scene has surrendered itself to the peripheral drama taking place between Cora and her exceedingly insubordinate fingers.

Rather than dutifully transcribing the turns of phrase dictated by Cora's thought, the rascals keep spurting out nonsense questions without even bothering to use the appropriate punctuation. Cora watches as a dense, single-spaced text block sculpts itself onto the page. The letters pile together in sequences she barely understands: Where is she. Where did she go. Can it be true. Who and what and where and when. How. Where is she. Where did she go. What will we do with an empty chair. An empty chair and an empty chair and an empty chair. Where did she go. Where did she go. Where did she go. Where did she go. Where did she go. Where did she go. Where did she go. Where did she go. Where. And where.

Cora protests. The phrases aren't even clever! And who can stomach such repetition? If you're going to go rogue, please at least type something mildly interesting. Cora is rather disgusted with the boredom of her own unconscious outpourings. And what exactly do you have against the question mark? Are you all really too lazy to bother depressing the Shift key once in a while? What a pathetic show you put on, hardly worth the price of the ticket! In a melodramatic flair, and with herself as only audience, Cora makes a show of dragging the mouse across the page in one overlong flourish. She'll show them. Watch this! Drag. Click. Enter. Then, gone. She wrests back control, removes her fingers from the keyboard, raises her voice to ask the question proper.

Susan's space seems just as quiet. The papers hold her eyes and mind with a fervor that makes Cora jealous. Come to think of it, Susan has been rather quiet this week. No morning news, very little discussion about the upcoming issue, not even a single story about her wayward son. Perhaps that's the reason. Has her son done something truly problematic, so much that it has put Susan in a more inward state of mind? Or worse, has Cora in some way slighted her, put her off accidentally with some offhand remark or question that got out of Cora's control? The goal shifts from Theresa's whereabouts to Susan's allegiance. Is she still on Cora's side? Cora's unwilling attack on the question mark notwithstanding, she must find out. Maybe it's the perfect opportunity to sleuth out Susan's state of mind *and* verify or discredit the rumor that Julie so insidiously forced upon her that night.

As if it suddenly occurs to her: Oh, I meant to ask you. Susan doesn't hear. Susan? A little louder. Susan. Susan looks up from her papers and says, I'm sorry, were you talking to me? Oh yes, sorry to interrupt. Just wondering, has there been any word from Theresa? It's been a few weeks now, so, yeah, just wondering. Susan's skin seems transparent in the morning light, almost cherubic with her blushed cheeks and plum-colored lips. She speaks in a cheerful, almost surprised tone that dispels Cora's fears of abandonment. Oh, I meant to tell you. Yes, sadly she called and officially quit. We're all fuzzy on the details, but it seems she's moving to Michigan. She already had a job lined up so who knows how long she's been planning the move. Cora exhales a response: Interesting. I had heard rumors but didn't want to draw conclusions until all the facts were in.

Good thing Theresa has already been ejected from the mainstream narrative. Good thing Cora has about a thousand things more pressing than a former friend's disappearance. Julie. The video store debacle. Chloe's health. A new apartment. All these desk papers that need to be graphed into quadrants and placed along opposite axes. How does it feel to move this pile here, or there, or perhaps relocate to the filing cabinet out of sight entirely? Susan's voice has thinned out the available air for breathing. The cursor blinks with innocent eyes.

Cora absorbs the blankness of the page. She readies herself to pollute it with justified words spaced to reach both margins. Now that things are settled, she can return to speeches of senators who need to be truncated and witness testimony that has gotten out of hand. The Shift key will have a fine time today after all!

As she ponders the relative merits of Backspace versus Delete, Cora's mind wanders unaccompanied into the video store. Why hadn't she gotten his name? It's a real travesty, one that could have been avoided with the proper safeguards in place. House Resolution number two hundred twelve: be it resolved that all video store employees henceforth shall be required to wear name tags for the purposes of mediating one Cora Freelene's ongoing quarrel with the question mark. Also, why had she lied? What could be the possible danger in simply telling him she had watched *Fitzcarraldo* years ago but had forgotten a good amount and wanted to re-watch? That's a perfectly reasonable thing for one to do in life, is it not? So why wouldn't those words come to mind when put on the spot of an afternoon? Maybe the rash has been clouding her good judgement. Or her worry for Chloe. This brief monologue entices Cora away from the truth, which calls back to her from down an adjacent path. Keep track of your deceits, Cora. Remember, the actual reason you rented the film was certainly not to re-watch it! Cora must admit that the truth is right in this case.

And what about lunch today with Julie? Cora had no choice but to agree, especially given the week's brilliant evasive maneuvers. One example: bringing coffee to work instead of passing by Julie to get to the break room. A genius-level tactic! That one took only a few sentences of explanation, conceived instantaneously when Julie asked about the change in pattern. Oh, I got tired of the awful break room coffee so I decided to brew my own in the mornings. Nothing to it! Even the truth can't deny that the break room coffee is terrible!

But never mind all of that. Cora has work to do. Her shoulders do a little shake for the ceremonial pivot before she dives into the lukewarm waters of abstraction. Productivity is up this week and the pace must be maintained at all costs. Just in the past few days, this month's issue gained abstracts on anti-drug campaigns, over-regulation of the automobile insurance industry, ecstasy use among millennial youth, asbestos and workplace safety, the increase in childhood leukemia near nu-

clear testing sites in Nevada, advancements in stem-cell research, and her personal favorite, The Product Packaging Pro-
tection Act, subtitled "Keeping Offensive Material Out of Our
Cereal Boxes."

Cora attempts to keep today's hearing from finding out
about her rather foul state of mind. Not only had she gotten
the Theresa news, not only does she have irritating lunchtime
plans, but now she faces down the most dastardly congressional deliberation of them all. The slender volume slumps on
the desk wanting to be innocuous but its all-caps title glares
out the inevitable. It never even had the chance to protest its
own contents! So there it sits, pregnant with the upper crust's
predilections toward cruelty. Cora opens the first page with
empathy. "Welfare and Marriage Issues" is the order of the
day, though the real topic is Congress's disdain for single
motherhood. Cora cracked that code long ago. She could write
the abstract with her eyes closed, and wishes they would let
her do it! But alas, the day will be full of exaltations for suburban nuclear families and undercurrents of blame for societal
decay on women. It's all there in the opening statement by
Rep. Wally Herger, Republication of California: he expresses
his "concern" for "families with children headed by women

with no husband present." His solution? Existing social support programs should be tied to support for two-parent families. Now this was really going to put a damper on Cora's spirits. She'd better not mention this to Julie, come to think of it. She'll never hear the end of admonitions to take action, to join organizations, to hold signs in the street. Cora knows herself too well. Her solution? Go home and cuddle with Chloe.

When the time comes to decide where to go for lunch, Cora mentions the egg salad sandwiches in the deli downstairs. Delicious. Moreover, proof that Theresa's absence means nothing. Julie is more than happy to accompany Cora downstairs. Of course. They chat on the way and Cora can't help but wish Julie could stop wanting things from her. All in all, Julie is okay. She's smart, rather pretty, a fair conversationalist, mildly interesting. Often annoying, but only when she comes around uninvited. A suitable friendly acquaintance and no more. But how is she supposed to know that?

It strikes Cora that she herself probably looks like all of these people downstairs in the café. Office workers. Business casual. Sitting across tables with colleagues discussing the goings on of the day. Unsettling! Would anyone know just by looking that none of it has anything to do with her? Nothing to do with great-grandmother's house or stockinged ladies or video tapes gathering dust? Or her falling body parts or the rubber band game? The lobster mug? The Merry Maid?

Julie's offer to pay for lunch was more than Cora could bear. That's even worse than trying to hold her hand in the elevator! Cora had pretended not to notice and moved to scratch her arm just at the right time. Had Julie felt the subterfuge? All these near misses force Cora to consider the ramifications of that night a couple of weeks ago. It hadn't been entirely unpleasant; on the contrary, Cora had enjoyed herself and, in a way, wouldn't mind that kind of evening again. If only it could end there. But no, Julie mistakes polarity for contact, a touch on the hand for a kiss! It occurs to Cora for a moment that Julie might actually care about her. But what could that mean? She doesn't know anything about Cora. She's never even met Chloe! How can she care when she knows so little? Or worse, does she think she knows more than she knows? Cora's thoughts dance to the white noise of the café until Julie's voice demands attention from across the table.

Bored with repetition, the conversation paces the length of the room just to feel itself move. Office politics. Changes in upper management. Protests taking place on the National

Mall. Julie suggests once again that they plan an inter-depart-mental party. Everyone would have so much fun, she says. Cora agrees and starts to plan an excuse for non-attendance. Does Cora want to go to a chamber concert at the National Gallery this weekend? No, there is still so much to do at great-grandmother's. Does Cora want a clutter-clearing companion? Julie thought the alliteration would sway public opinion. Sweet of you to offer but no, the last stage of the process in-volves decisions the grandparents need to make so there's re-ally not much Julie could do to help. Another master stroke of circumvention!

Cora feels the color of the world change once she reaches the safety of her cubicle. Before lunch, everything was a sod-den yellow; now, it's rusted orange. A minor shift, but enough to support the theory of parallel universes. Cora's weight has bent the timeline so it points slightly more eastward. New pos-sibilities span the horizon, all events previous to this moment are immediately irrelevant in the world. In short, Cora decides to make a change. Julie will never understand, but that hardly warrants the labor of abstraction. After all, Cora herself only vaguely understands, so shouldn't energy focus on that corner of the night sky? Figure things out first, Cora, and then clean up the mess.

As soon as she sits in her trusty black chair, Cora immediately feels herself rise in the direction of Adam's section of the building. Will he be up for a quick chat? Only one way to find out. Adam is there, working, but looks up promptly to catch Cora's attention. It's the correct behavior for a distraction and Cora rewards him with her charm. Slaving away over lunch, are we? Well that simply won't do. Adam mumbles something about a deadline but Cora isn't listening. It's been a while since we had a good catch up. How about we chat over lunch tomorrow? Cora doesn't know what she's saying. We could go downstairs, they have great egg salad sandwiches. It'll be on me, in fact! Cora's words take the train to a different station. They're on the track, there they go! No catching them now. Sounds great, she hears from behind a grey wall. I'll be there. Perfect, see you then! It's the album's last note. Cora walks away irritated at his lack of hesitation. He didn't even give her a second to think it through!

198 / SARAH D'STAIR

THE RETURN HOME GREETS Cora with a door thump to Chloe's patient body. Chloe, how long have you been waiting at the door for me? My poor, sweet Chloe. I'm sorry I was gone so long. It's Thursday of a long week. Only one more day, I promise! If only Cora could stay home with Chloe every day, if only she never had to leave great-grandmother's! They could play and cuddle and sleep and mostly just exist in the same room together, each doing whatever strikes them at the moment. Chloe could sleep; Cora could read. Chloe could eat morsels in gravy; Cora could order in every night. Chloe could sleep some more; Cora could wander the house, thinking in the quiet. At night they could nestle together in the old chair and watch Judge Scheindlin put the night sky in order.

Eventually the hugging stops and Cora is left alone with her body. It is trying to tell her something but she can't decipher the message. Hunger? No. Illness? No. Some kind of discomfort, though, right? Yes, some kind. The sparkled yellow chair offers her a thinking spot. Definite tension in the neck and back, but that's not quite it. Likely an overwhelming atrophy. Yes, but no, not exactly. Suddenly the right answer runs its fingers through Cora's hair. A shower! That's what she needs.

Grimy skin, oily face, sweaty hands. All of them remind Cora that she woke too late this morning to clean herself. Eureka! Evening showers are wonders of the world. No pressure to leave sooner than when the warm water runs out, and afterward, a walk through steamy rooms. Cora cranks up great-grandmother's A/C on her way to the bathroom to make sure the house can breathe.

The bodily relics are there, waiting for Cora, private citizens caught in a network of governmental oversight. The cup. The tape. Ten hanging pictures of a rash secured in plastic bags. All of it scientific evidence only when someone turns around to look. Particles are that way, too, at least that's the going theory. At any rate, Cora's information gathering campaign has been a success overall. The pictures show a progressive reddening over the course of one week, and then a gradual pinkening that coincides remarkably with Cora's decision to the use creme she had purchased at the drug store.

What would people say if they found out what was hidden in the cup? The question rises in the thickening steam and trails off into the hallway. No matter. All she needs to do is keep people out, which on the whole isn't a difficult job. She only needs to say No. These delicate archives must be kept tight in the vault, climate-controlled, access restricted. In fact, these artifacts would be the only proof of her existence if indeed great-grandmother's house *is* eating her alive. Small remnants of her chemical decomposition. XY equals X Y.

A shower list begins almost as soon as the water runs over Cora's back. Things to do, in order. First, shower. Done. Second, change out Chloe's water bowls, which all seem determined to live under a surface layer of dust. Third, the house. More specifically, books. An earlier glance revealed nothing of major interest on either of the three bookshelves, but still, someone should organize the volumes into well-considered piles.

A list of three isn't bad, but also seems rather paltry. Surely one more thing to do can be found! How long can three bookshelves take? The voice of moderation shows up late to the party but nonetheless reminds Cora that she might consider taking one thing at a time. Just a thought, not meaning to press. Cora's reluctance responds in the affirmative but with a surreptitious roll of the eyes.

Perhaps the more immediate concern should be this business with the body. Cora's mind is on the countertop. What can she start collecting now that the rash has nearly healed?

It'd be lazy to forgo the gallery show just when the collection's getting interesting. After a few minutes, an idea finds Cora while she's annoyed at the amount of water accumulating in the tub. It's the drain cover's fault, or more precisely, the fault of all the hair that's caught there. How much hair is Cora losing these days? More than normal? What's normal anyway when it comes to hair loss in the shower? Is great-grandmother's house once again finding her too delicious to resist?

What Cora needs is a point of comparison, a methodology to ascertain a judgement. Her shower thoughts turn to words for the scientific method. Control group. Sample size. Independent variable. Here is the plan. Collect all lost hair over the course of one week from all possible sources: drain, brush, clothes, floor. Collect again the next week and compare. Think of the line graph that would make! Trends over time caught in the trap of the x and y axis! Zero to sixty! Superfluity to necessity in less than a minute!

The water eventually runs cold so it is time to let the thinking stop. Cora dries her feet and shins for Chloe's post-shower nuzzle, then prepares herself for the commencement. First, a tissue gathers the clump of hair in the drain catcher, a good amount but not terribly concerning. Next, she empties the hairbrush and adds it to the pile. The floor has the pesky tendency to collect both Cora's and Chloe's hair without discrimination so it's going to have to wait. Besides, it's a nice pile of hair so far. Not bad for a day's work. It looks only mildly grotesque, not at all as bad as she had imagined. Still, it'd likely do better in a cup of some sort. A cup to match the other! She knows just where to find it now that the kitchen countertops are organized.

The specimen's perfect fit at the bottom of the plastic cup makes Cora feel healthy and systematic. She might even fit the word 'accomplished' into the sentence! Now on to the next item on the agenda: Chloe's water. No problem! Cora is on a roll tonight, there's no telling how much she'll get done!

A brief glance at a few of the bowls leads to a change in plans. Delightful Chloe had dropped several of Cora's stray hair bands into her water, a game she plays often though Cora has never figured out why. Most of the time it's hair bands, but sometimes Cora finds socks, gloves, cat toys – pretty much anything mouth-sized that Chloe finds laying around. Cora takes the discovery as a sign that Chloe wants to play. Cora flings the small band down the hall and Chloe follows at full attack. She hunches nearby, waits at the ready to chase it down again. Cora surprises her with a new direction. Chloe catches sight and barrels down toward the living room. This game has lasted her whole life. They know it like clockwork.

Great-grandmother's little house has become rather inhospitable to Chloe's all out sprints. The papers and towel experiment had not gone as planned and now it's all strewn across the hallway floor. Chloe has to dart in and out of accumulated piles all over the house. Should the hallway take priority this evening? Maybe the piles can be moved right back into the third bedroom, but more neatly to keep the organizational pattern. On the other hand, the move seems like it would take a long time and Chloe wants to play right now. Cora does the only sensible thing. She removes the towels to expose the papers underneath, delicately pushes each pile against the wall, and creates an airstrip of clear carpet all the way down the hall. Now Chloe has a place to run and the papers haven't entirely lost their coherence. They can be sorted again later, if needed. At the moment, though, the joy of seeing Chloe exercise and jump and hide is more than enough to keep Cora satisfied.

After ten minutes, Chloe is sufficiently exhausted, and Cora must move on to the next task at hand. The water dishes take thirty minutes to empty and fill one by one. Maybe there are a few too many. One in each room would be satisfactory, wouldn't it? Perhaps, but what is really being argued here? Is Chloe's well-being not worth thirty minutes on a Thursday evening? Preposterous!

Cora needs to make some real headway this evening. No getting around it. It's time to start making some decisions. Great-grandmother's bookshelves exist in two dimensions, flattened images from Cora's childhood memory. The books had never moved, never switched places with each other, no addition or subtraction to revise their numbers. Cora herself rarely touched the books growing up. They taught her very early the beauty of stasis.

Now Cora must touch them all. Disrupt the tableau, vanish the mirage. But first, the house begs for music. In the living room, Cora gives a quick Hello to the women and dolls, then searches for just the right sound to lighten the mood. Pat Boone and Lawrence Welk seem just the right flavor. "Moody River" is one of her favorites. She puts a record on and keeps the other in queue, hoping the haunting lyrics will be audible from the back of the house. She tells the volume not to mind itself tonight.

As soon as she pulls the first title from the shelf Cora knows she is doing the right thing. These books want to be held, perused, leafed through, coddled. She can hardly tell where her hands end and the pages begin. The first is in a series of backyard birding guides, though no memory comes to mind of great-grandmother talking about birds. A coffee-table book about marble collecting, a few about rare coins, one on techniques for needlepoint. The next shelf down begins the true intrigue. Mostly very old children's books, ones that must have been saved from grandmother's childhood. She had brothers, which explains the proliferation of books for young boys. A writer named F.W. Dixon is well-represented: *Tom Swift in the Caves of Ice*, *The Sinister Sign Post*, *The Hidden Harbor Mysteries*, *The Secret of the Caves*, and Cora's favorite title, *The Missing Chums*. Faded yellow-beige covers have held tight to these secrets for decades. Grosset and Dunlap, Publishers would be proud. The reference section at the college library must have an index of defunct publishers. Cora will have to look them up one day.

The Hardy Boys have solved mysteries on these shelves for years as well, alongside the Bobbsey Twins' tales about Meadowbrook and Blueberry Island. *The Adventures of Tom*

Sawyer is the only book Cora sees as truly literary, and in fact, a distinct memory of reading the white washing scene comes to mind. Other delightful titles pour themselves into Cora's willing intellect: *Mrs. Wiggs at the Cabbage Patch*, *Wagons to the Wilderness*, *Gene Autry and the Redwood Pirates*, *The Duke of Plaza Tora*. Another of her favorites is simply called *The Glob*, which seems an intellectual property hearing waiting to happen in its eerie similarity to *The Blob*.

The book task requires a discipline that Cora is lacking. Five minutes perusing every book would mean a lot of minutes! The additive property strikes again. Categorize, box. That's all there is to it. No need to investigate the contents of each volume. Except this one. *Tall Tales of America*. Blue cover, tattered corners. Published in 1958 by Guild Press, Inc. and edited by Irwin Shapiro. An oversized Paul Bunyan grins like a proud father on the cover, axe in one hand, full-sized pine tree in the other. Before him, a blue ox, yoked, with pained, half-closed eyes. The words inside tell stories of subjugation. Pecos Bill roping a tornado with bare hands and tanning a lion with a snake used as a whip. Gruesome pictures illustrate the feats. Old Stormalong's bare hands subdue a whale. Iron worker Joe Magarac uses his hands as ladles for molten steel.

Johnny Appleseed turns forests into farms. One of the final stories recounts the amazing feats of Sam Patch, who can't subdue anything, but who can for some reason survive a fall from any height. The picture shows his jump from Niagara Falls. Cora files the collection under A for Antipathy and leaves to switch the record. A tiredness comes over her. Maybe it's time to take a rest.

THE METRO TRAIN IS hobbled with thought. Yoked oxen, North American bird species, the skins of lions. Apple trees. Childhood mysteries. Would she know the names of family members who read any of the books in great-grandmother's house? Or have they been entirely forgotten? Most likely forgotten. Cora often feels that her family belongs to someone else. Avoidance is her namesake, which is slightly foolish because they really are quite nice to her.

It only occurs to her when the train pulls into her station that she agreed to accompany Adam to lunch today. Agreed to accompany him? Don't forget who invited whom! In the vast category of heterological words, Cora's full name sits front and center. She doesn't even apply to herself. In fact, Cora would rather be ill at home than suffer the consequences of her own invitation. Or she'd rather spend all day with the longest and most boring omnibus bill Congress has ever considered. What could live on the opposite side of this particular greater-than sign? What about lunch with Julie? Would she prefer that to lunch with Adam? Just like that, she's solved the equation. Decidedly, no. The train belches her out onto the platform, annoyed by her lack of cohesion.

Settled in at work, Cora decides to write the best abstract she has ever written in her life. Really get it right this time, right words in the right order. Right, right, right. Flush to the margins, column by column of perfect text. "From Research to Practice: Improving America's Schools in the 21st Century" will learn to appreciate Cora's precision knife skills, her deference, her domination.

Each abstract is a glorious puzzle with the fate of the world at stake in its solution. The earth will either be set exactly right, magnetic poles just far enough apart and at a proper distance from the sun to support life. Or it will just miss the mark, plunging all of life into an eternal oblivion from which it will never recover. Perhaps a bit dramatic, but Cora doesn't mind.

First, the opening statement, generally a performance for future constituents a congressperson wants to assuage. The niceties can be ignored, the salutations and apologies for events that caused tardiness or disarray. Then, the real work starts. Opening statements, witness introductions, facts and figures and anecdotal evidence. An ivy league professor of education first outlines the negative effects of relying solely on standardized test results for school funding decisions. The statement itself holds no interest to Cora, who, for better or worse, has little interest in standardized testing or school funding procedures. But then the adventure begins. Cora must scoop up words by the armful and sort them out into truth. How to begin the phrase: Negative effects? Detriments caused by? Detriments of? Or she can take another route altogether. Make standardized testing the subject, allow the predicate to waste away behind it. Standardized testing's negative impact on... Except Cora hates apostrophes. They render phrases lazy, ugly. So then, standardized testing goes at the end. But what are the impacts, exactly? Does this distinguished gentleman talk about one in particular for more than ten pages? Here, he discusses inequities in testing formats for students with disabilities for one, two, three, four, five, six pages. Not enough for its own phrase, but how can she justify leaving it out alto-gether? Some education researchers in the coming years may want to know that this witness outlined this set of concerns. So, a puzzle of incorporation. Negative effects on students, including students with disabilities, of standardized testing as an indicator of school funding decisions. Indicator. Not quite right. Negative effects on students, including students with disabilities, of standardized testing as a criterion for school funding. Criterion. Yes! That's exactly right. But does he dis-cuss only funding, or is the testimony more about academic and social outcomes of testing for various groups of students? The mystery deepens, complexities become unruly exponents in need of a number. With each word she orders and reorders, considers and reconsiders. Words are put on hold for later, placed to the side and replaced when opportunity calls. She indulges in the most elegant ones and unabashedly eradicates the others when they no longer serve. The good ones carry her to heights and accept their places in the celestial sphere. Sense. Logic. Idea. Intent. Cora is symphonic conductor of syllables and sounds, tamer of outliers and goddess of all that is order. She holds the center in compressed, economical turns of phrase. The earth itself spins toward obedience and a reverent curtsey. Cora, mastermind of language and all that is primal in time and mind.

The abstract works itself to perfection before the noon hour. Lunchtime. This is what Cora gets for instigating. A fall from the heavens, peace to panic, her silent workspace to the grating noise downstairs! The inevitable stares her down and she responds with a daydream. A quiet corner, a nineteenth-century novel. Or a travel journal about Provence or Paris. As the moment approaches, even lunch with Julie seems preferable. At least Julie doesn't mind if Cora speaks very little. Or the dream of all dreams, to be home playing with Chloe. The digital clock defends her fantasies until the very last minute.

She gathers her purse and money and prepares for the hour ahead. Eyebrows and a cheery demeanor, political jargon, questions Cora is supposed to answer. Maybe it will be enjoyable in some way, at the very least a worthwhile diversion from Julie's interference. The two women need an honest discussion, but that means Cora would have to suffer Julie's emotions.

Adam arrives a few minutes early, says he has come to fetch her. Fetch. Charming enough, Cora supposes, but certainly not impressive. He asks about her day, how Susan is getting along with her move to management. This development of a few days ago had bored Cora to the point of forgetting. Oh, we haven't really talked about it. We've both been buried in work for the next issue since we're an abstractor short. Adam nods in sympathy. A side thought follows Cora down the elevator. Will Susan leave her desk to sit in another office? What a bother. What a bothersome thought to bother Cora on a lunch that's already a bother! The word is getting indulgent so Cora changes the subject.

The busy café punches Cora with unreasonable decibels. Voices low and shrill and unnecessarily chatty sit around metallic bistro tables that amplify the din. Time to settle in for a long lunch. At least Adam tries to amuse her by poking fun at nearby customers. A woman with mismatched socks. A man with a piece of cookie in his mustache. Giggling young girls who believe they are relevant. True observations, but not profound. Cora returns a decent performance of squinting laughs and rolling eyes.

Lunch takes a turn when Adam begins talking about golf. Apparently, Cora has gone to lunch with a person who is also a former golf champion. In younger days, he says, though he's probably not yet thirty. His golf career now is largely amateur, weekend tee times and giving a few lessons here and there. Cora for some reason feels appalled. What do you mean younger days? You can't be past thirty, surely you can get back on your game! His laughter informs Cora that her statement is well-meaning but uninformed.

The remaining forty-five minutes give Cora a foundational course on all things golf. Names of various clubs and when to use them, backswing, downswing, fairway and fore, eagle, birdie, ace. A true primer. Cora appreciates the aesthetic of the words themselves but feels sorry they got stuck with such anodyne meanings.

The egg salad in her chewing mouth begins to go dry as she concentrates on feigned interest. Asking appropriate questions. Matching body language to a reasonable extent. An idea comes to her which is on a different subject but she dutifully sends it packing. Cora has learned the hard way that some people only enjoy talking about themselves. It's not a bad trait. The more he talks, the more Cora's joys and stories can stay right where they belong, as secrets told only to Chloe and guarded with tissue and tape.

Cora is a script he has written and she plays the part well. She doesn't miss a single line and says them all with gusto! A page turn obscures the next bit of dialogue until it's too late but the show must go on. Do you want to join me for a few holes tomorrow morning? The weather's supposed to be beautiful, not too warm. The first few holes have a nice view of the Potomac. Cora delivers her line right on cue. Yeah, sure, that sounds nice. It's a date.

HOME AGAIN. CHLOE AT the door. A little more distressed than usual. Did something happen today, Chloe? Strange noises? A knock at the door? Cora briefly panics that perhaps the grandparents made a visit while she was at work. The thought is unbearable given the state of things at first glance. No, they would have called first. They may be pushy, but they aren't rude.

Music. That's what the house needs right now. Music will lighten the mood and let Chloe know she's not alone. It's Friday night and they have nowhere to be, no one to see, nothing to do except put items in boxes. Before she changes into her comfortable clothes, Cora searches for the evening's soundtrack. Perry Como, Ed Ames, Guy Lombardo, some Smothers Brothers in case she and Chloe want to hear voices. Cora joins the room in thanks for great-grandmother's taste in records.

Cora showers to the tune of dim melodies, their sounds muted by the clash of falling water. Competing soundwaves uncloak above Cora's head. She imagines them in an epic battle for her attention, a bloodbath, a vast, deep chaos across a clearcut field. It's a wonder anyone survives!

Thankful for Chloe's unconcerned presence, Cora turns off the faucet and gives the music notes a win. No time to negotiate a cease-fire, she has work to do, books to sort and maybe some clothing to pack up in the bedroom. Chloe curls up and rolls on the bathroom mat while Cora dries herself. Adorable. And distracting! Chloe, your charm almost made me forget! Diligent researcher, Cora remembers to collect samples from the shower and hairbrush. After only two days, the cup is filled a quarter of the way. A fair amount of hair, all things considered. Perhaps it's not in Cora's imagination after all.

After her shower, a little bit of dinner, and a few minutes playing with Chloe, Cora sets to work on the last bookshelf to be organized. Her system, indisputable genius, leads to numerous stacks of books arranged by theme in different areas of the house. When the time comes to donate, there will be no need for even a second glance! Geography has taken care of it all. Hobby books in the third bedroom. Novels in the back bedroom. Children's books in the living room. The collected works of Louise Mühlbach get a spot of their own tucked away next to great-grandmother's chair. Fascinating, this woman. German or Scandinavian. How many books did she write? Here are thirteen but how many more are there? What a life to lead, writing historical fiction in the nineteenth century only for an insignificant Cora to find them a century later buried on an ancestral shelf.

The *Tall Tales* book from yesterday haunts the living room, the enslaved ox, the mutilated tree. Just a glance plunges Cora into despair for all creatures who must suffer human beings. Chloe, do you suffer me? The question can't bear to know its own answer. Paul Bunyan soon finds himself buried under Anne of Green Gables where he belongs.

Children's books of all kinds occupy the last few shelves to explore. Bizarre images. Smiling dogs in school desk chairs eager to answer teacher's question. Daffy Duck in a space suit. Mean, snickering cats. Tootle and Scuffy, Doctor Dan. Little Golden Books, cozy and full of memories. One more book before lights out, pretty please? Piano keys. Silky ends of blankets.

Robert Louis Stevenson's *A Child's Garden of Verses*, rusty red and in fairly good repair, topples from the shelf into Cora's hands. The cursive inscription reads "Christmas 1936." 1936! Marvelous. Could this have been a gift for grandmother, her small fingers clutching it next to the Christmas tree? It looks well-loved, crayoned pages and spill marks inside. Cora never knew Stevenson even wrote children's poetry. Curious. What did old R.L. give to the children of the western world? Cora leafs through pages, unsurprised to find poems called "My Bed Is a Boat" and "Happy Thought" and "From a Railway Carriage." Some titles amuse more than others: "Auntie's Skirts" and "The Dumb Soldier." All in all, the verse is rather forced, uninteresting, boring. Cloying. Saccharine! The word is almost too good to waste on the book. Cora's generosity saves the whole thing from utter disgrace, along with the lucky fact that it was written for children. She blushes for poetry's sake.

Her general contempt having run its course, Cora spends a few minutes searching for any redeemable lines. She finds several scattered here and there. Some, she admits, are quite lovely. Still, no regrets. A few good lines do not equal a book of poetry! Snobbishness aside, it'd be a shame to let these superior lines wither away in a book of bad verse. Let's rescue them, shall we, Chloe? Cora finds a medical bill with a blank back page that seems happy to help in the cause. A heroic transcriptionist, Cora removes the words from their contexts and places them into hers: "Now we beyond the embers flee" and "Happy chimney-corner days." "See the greater swallows pass." "And warmly on the roof it looks, and flickers on the backs of books." "Shines in the ivies on the garden wall with the black night overhead." And her favorite: "These are the hills, these are the words – these are my starry solitudes." The paper is too congruent so Cora rips it into strips around each phrase. Refrigerator magnets enlist themselves to help, they beam with pride at what they get to hold.

While admiring her feat of poetic license, Cora notices in the periphery that Chloe has taken a seat at the dining room table. On the dining table, more precisely. Sweet Chloe. Her paw reaches out tentatively toward one of great-grand-mother's glass tumblers. Head cocked, curious. Of course. That's why Cora had meant to move them last night! Too many of life's complications, all at once, no wonder she had lapsed in her duty. Adorable, but ill-advised.

Before Cora can call for a halt, down the glass goes, a long fall to the linoleum, now in geometric shards from here to doomsday. Cora springs into action. She scoops Chloe up from the table, puts her in their bedroom and closes the door so she's safe inside. Then she sweeps up the fragments, runs a wet cloth across the floor, and walks across every square inch barefoot to test the surface. Not a sliver left. Chloe is safe.

The trash can, overflowing with takeout, can't hold the contents of the dust bin. Of course, it's always something! Cora finds a willing box and gently pours in the broken glass. Just for now. She'll throw it away properly tomorrow. She closes the lid tight to keep Chloe out, and makes her way to the back of the house. Nothing to it, Chloe. Wasn't that a fun adventure for you? Pet, purr, pet, purr. Now, let's get back to work.

BEFORE LEAVING THE NEXT morning to meet Adam at the golf course, Cora calls Julie and apologizes for being so evasive. Sometimes she just doesn't know what she's doing, she gets a bit anxious and withdraws. No, you haven't done anything wrong. Promise. It's just a stressful time and who knew we'd end up getting together? Cora is skilled at such speeches. She has had a lot of practice. Her methodology is always organizational. Julie in Theresa's place. Adam in Julie's. Shuffle, shuffle, shuffle. Arrange. Rearrange.

She meets Adam within the hour. He is quite confident that Cora will enjoy golfing once she's given it a chance. She nods an affable smile. He doesn't know she already has an exit strategy. She has her car, as always. Cora rarely allows others to drive her anywhere, just in case. Adam will learn in a moment that the grandparents called late last night to announce an unexpected visit this morning. She didn't want to miss golfing, though, so she thought she could still get in a few holes. Aren't you proud of the way golf terminology just rolls off my tongue? Cora dazzles. He thinks she's gone out of her way to spend time with him. Cora comes out unscathed and he is none the wiser!

He asks, Do you like my golfer's cap? It makes me look like an old man. Cora laughs and says it looks cute. He introduces her to the different clubs, says she can use the ones he bought for his mother. He shows her how to grip and how to swing. Cora admits she enjoys the cool morning air and sunshine. She tells him she wishes she could stay longer. Sadly, she needs to

leave after probably the first three holes. Adam seems understanding but she knows he's also annoyed. She says she'll
walk back to the car and he can continue with the course. He
insists on taking her back in the cart.

Cora isn't lying about the sun. It is, in fact, refreshing to be
outdoors. However, can the sun tell Cora what she is doing out
here? No, it cannot. It's a giant sphere full of failure in that
respect so let's not get too excited. Animosity travels the arc
of her golf swing. A pathetic attempt. This is going to take
forever. Maybe she'll leave after two holes. Or one! She's in
a play by Ionesco, absurdity has caught her in its grip. It's
throwing the rubber band down the hall for her to chase, un-
raveling her like one of Chloe's strings. Cora runs back and
forth down the long hallway for the crowd's amusement and
only stops when she gets to the green. Cora hasn't approved
the patterns in the grass, or this particular ray of sunlight.
Adam swings. Smiles. Puts a ball in the little hole. Says See,
that's how you do it. Cora loses a ball in the dirt. Laughs. Ridiculous. The Potomac is lovely this time of year. Yes, it really
is. Cora is lost on the fairway, an irrational number searching
for a place on the number line.

It's only three holes. She can do this. Adam is perfectly nice, even fun. He's making it as enjoyable as he can, and to be fair, he has no idea what she's thinking. Awkwardness. Even misery. She tells him a joke of self-deprecation, pokes fun at him in good humor. Says it's a beautiful day, thanks him for getting her out of the house. Maybe she'll practice so they can play a real game someday. All of this with absolute credulity. Adam is Paul Bunyan with his axe. Cora, the oxen yoked and blue.

Cora manages to end the performance with a convincing speech about how sorry she is to be leaving early. Rematch soon? Yes, definitely. She leans in for a polite hug and feels his lips brush her own. He waves as she drives away. Cora blasts The Beatles, blinded, looks ahead to the street signs that lead her back to great-grandmother's, Chloe, books, bowls, the girl and the women and the clothes in perfect patterns on the bed.

The chair and sofa and dining room table have remained where Cora left them. Chloe nestles with the dolls, content with a slow blink of greeting. The rest of Saturday. There is much to do. Build boxes and secure them with tape, sort and then put items in the boxes. It all feels meandering, useless,

Sisyphus up the hill. Maybe Chloe will play hide and seek, the boxes placed on their sides. She'll pounce as Cora passes by pretending not to notice. This game has lasted for hours in the past. Maybe it will again.

The house begs for music again to sooth its melancholy. Perry Como is on the top of the pile so Cora plays the record. Comforting, his voice. Grown up. Self-assured. Boxes will get filled today. Books and papers will disappear into them. The rooms will get empty.

Cora checks again on her rash, nearly healed but still pinkish around her middle. The cream had done the trick. One day, the only evidence that it existed will get packed away too. Maybe she should just do it now, get it over with. But it's not time. Once the rash has entirely disappeared from her body, maybe then. For now, best to finish out the cycle. The Polaroid clicks and whirrs, adds another picture to the collage.

A thin layer of dust had once again settled on the water in Chloe's bowls and cups. It must have been the books. Time to swap it out. She really should keep better track of which dishes Chloe uses. Maybe two or three fewer dishes wouldn't make a difference. Next time she's at the store she'll buy a notebook solely devoted to documenting Chloe's water intake. Draw a schematic. Write down numbers from a ruler.

Ferrying water to and from the kitchen, another of Cora's brilliant ideas to animate the scene. It's lucky, too, because things were beginning to feel stagnant. Time to invigorate the day! Every time Cora returns to the kitchen sink to fill another bowl, those endearing scraps of paper stare at her with such joy and poetry. Such a shame for them to be stuck on a fridge door. That's no place for sentiments like "my starry solitudes"! They should get prime real estate, hung in all the places Cora sees most often. One next to great-grandmother's chair. Another by the front door. A few in the living room and more in the bedroom. Maybe even one in the bathroom. Genius remedy! Poetry etched in her own hand, all around the house!

Perry Como sings with another gentleman while Cora hangs and re-hangs "See the greater swallows pass" so the semi-nude women can see the words. "May…be, you'll think ..of me.. when you..are all..a..lone." Cora's spirits swirl around in the song. Her thoughts swirl with her. He's writing a novel. A novel! "May…be, you'll sit..and sigh.. wishing..that I..were near." What could it mean, this novel, and had she found her way into his words somehow? If she could, she'd pull him right up to the front of the sentence, no predicate for him! Even if he didn't cover ten pages, she'd still find a way to sneak him in.

In that moment, Cora vows never to return *Fitzcarraldo*. Even if it never leaves its spot on top of great-grandmother's television, even if it gathers a foot of dust and hundreds in late fees. He will have to ask for it every time she visits. Tell her it's overdue, threaten to cancel her membership, eject her from the store, charge her to replace the video which he warns her will not be cheap. She will make excuses. She'll say she just can't stop watching it, over and over and over. She'll ask him to renew it, pretty please, just one more time. She'll make him choose: Cora or store policy. He'll have to choose her. He'll start to make excuses for her, say to himself how impressed he is with her taste in cinema. Maybe he'll even pay the fees without telling her! Klaus Kinski's wild hair will draw them together. They'll dream of steamboats and opera in the misty moonlight!

PART SIX

CORA AND CHLOE HAVE been playing the tail game on the living room floor for at least ten minutes. Chloe started it this time, without question Cora plays along. Chloe's tail flicks and flutters across pages of the Apartment Guide, which Cora dutifully reads while spread out next to little white flowers that hop along the rims of eight matching bowls. Chloe makes a racket with the thwapping of her tail and Cora responds with a finger thwap of equal measure just alongside. Chloe thwaps again and Cora's ready fingers jump to it, this time brushing Chloe's tail with the lightest of touch. Chloe bristles her tail then brings it down with a thump onto Cora's hand. Cora pins Chloe's tail down for the splittest seconds, then lets it go so Chloe can thwap three more times. Thwap thwap thwap. Quick and on purpose. Cora onomatopoeias the moment as Chloe's tail and her own fingers dance and prance and seek and find each other. The darkening room doesn't seem to care, it goes on with its dimming light, goes on with its old melodies and dozens of pairs of eyes. Cora and Chloe give the eyes a lovely show and they smile or smirk or sneer from the surface of their faces. Blue innocent eyes, seductive brown eyes, piercing ones and faded ones and eyes that open and close by themselves when baby is held flat. Cora forgets who is on display for whom, or considers perhaps they're all each other's ephemera, trinkets caught up on a dusty shelf waiting to be forgotten.

Chloe's disregard for the Apartment Guide mirrors the non-chalance of the women on the wall. Everyone is unconcerned except Cora, who had begun to fret and worry after the last talk with the grandparents. Two weeks. That's all we have left, Chloe. Two weeks! Remember, I told you Monday night we would find an apartment. Well tonight's the night and what kind of help have you been? Cora gives Chloe a kiss on the belly. Ravenous purr. Chloe's arms hug Cora's head in close.

A hundred glossy pages suffer Cora's dismissal before real-izing their own inadequacy. Cora falls in love with the word parameters and the variety of sounds a vowel can make. The place has to accept pets, naturally, and ideally without a monthly upcharge. It can't be too far from work, but also not too close. Proximity to the red line is paramount. It must have a view of a field and trees and squirrels and birds for Chloe. It can't be too expensive or too loud or too large or too small. It must have wall-to-wall carpet and a window sufficient for Chloe's long days at home without Cora. A sliding glass door, therefore, is a necessity. A fireplace would be nice, and room for all her books. Maybe enough space for some of great-grandmother's belongings, her chair and sparking yellow dining table, the records, the dolls, the pictures. Cora has enough money saved for a bigger place if she plans it just right. There'd be no harm, even the grandparents couldn't complain! Geometric proofs line up rank and file on the living room floor with Cora.

Two weeks. How will we find something just right in two weeks, Chloe? Maybe we should ask the grandparents for a bit more time, just another week or so to finish things out. But then they might start asking questions, or show up unannounced. Or worse, they'd say no and that would be the end of the line. No, Chloe, we need to face the music. Figure things out.

Speaking of music, how about some Bobby Darin this evening to velveteen the mood? Cora hops up from the floor and gives Chloe a quick pet before sorting through records. We really should alphabetize these someday. Imagine, D for Darin! S for Streisand, C for Cline, B for Boone and The Buffalo Bills! If there's one thing we'll do before we leave, Chloe, it's alphabetize great-grandmother's records. Maybe that'll be on the docket for tonight, a real triumph of democratic civility. It's rather pointless to be looking for apartments at this time of night anyway, since all the offices are closed.

Cora joins Chloe again on the floor near the sofa. Pointless seems to be the word of the night, Chloe. Long, slow blink. Kiss kiss. Pet pet. Cora looks around to make sense of her surroundings. Kitchen items, sorted. Books, piled by genre. Plates, bowls and cups, matched. Dolls, arranged. Knick-knacks, counted to twenty-five. The little girl, appeased. What more could be done at this point, without packing it all away unbearably out of sight? Cora might as well pack herself away if it comes to that, wrapped and boxed and neat as a pin. Besides, who in their right mind can endure the loneliness of an empty room? Chloe, it's just going to have to wait, the boxes and the tape. Save it for the last minute. The system we've developed over time is a perfect diagrammatic blueprint for just such an activity. The floor and countertops will take at most a day to sort and pack, don't you think? And we have two weeks! Practically an eternity. Two weeks is like a year in Cora time, with her uncanny periods of hyper-productivity, especially when put on the spot. How many complicated abstracts can she write in two weeks? At least two a day, and sometimes three. At five days in a week, that's at least ten or fifteen congressional hearings sliced and diced with perfect accuracy, and right within the margins! Nothing to it, Chloe. Next week the boxes will get their fill. For now, let's help these records claim their birthright among the capital letters.

Just as the first few albums find their way to the floor for sorting, Cora realizes she hasn't brought in great-grand-mother's mail today. In fact, it may have been a week since she last checked the mail. Likely nothing of interest, but still, the mailbox can get filled to overflowing with all the catalogs and mailers that tend to arrive in steady rhythm each day. The records can wait a few minutes.

The humid evening wraps itself around Cora's loose black t-shirt and lounge shorts as soon as she walks outside. No cars, little noise, an uneasy peace, like shadowy corners from an old noir film. Cora collects a handful of papers and begins to sort them on the way back into the house. Coupons, local papers, credit card offers for great-grandmother. Nothing of

234 / SARAH D'STAIR

note. Except, peeking out between two grocery store circulars is the corner of what looks like a postcard. Cora pulls it out from hiding, and there it is, an autumnal college scene with the words Ann Arbor followed by a rather precocious exclamation point. Ann Arbor, Michigan! Theresa. A short message is jotted on the back: "Sorry I disappeared. Nathan got a job at the college so I decided to come with. Things got away. Miss you. Come visit!"

Come visit? Come visit. Cora is the subject of a subject-less sentence, an imperative without the imperative, followed by another annoying exclamation point. One isn't enough for a single postcard? And Nathan. Nathan? She writes his name like Cora already knows it! A quirky nineteen-fifties swimming pool gets in return a generic picture of northern foliage. Doubt vanishes between the trees. Chloe, we have been slighted. Theresa must be punishing us for not calling, for sending a few cursory phrases after so many years of adjectives. How long had they known each other, two years? And it comes to this, an exchange of abstracts written by hand and a name given without a single word of context? Cora will never know now what it all means. We'll never know, Chloe. Come visit? What a silly thing for her to suggest! Ten years, a lifetime has passed since Theresa's departure. An historical epoch. An eon! So much has happened since then. How could Theresa know that Cora hardly thinks about her anymore? Not enough to write back, and certainly not enough to visit.

Despite its affirmed meaninglessness, the postcard nonetheless changes the color of the day. A bit darker, a reddish shade of shame. Cora should have called. Left a message, at least behaved like a person who knows how to do life. A postcard? What was she thinking? What were we thinking, Chloe? At least it's a pretty picture of the college, noncommittal, innocuous. Not altogether unpleasant. At the very least, confirmation that Theresa exists. Cora hangs the card on the refrigerator in the space vacated by Robert Louis Stevenson and promptly puts the Theresa narrative to the side. It's time to return to the living room. These albums won't alphabetize themselves.

Cora sits on the floor and folds the task into her evening. A few dozen capital letters need her taxonomic skill and she vows to offer them her full and complete attention. Some get placed before or after others in just the right order, but all in all, Cora is uninspired. She looks at Chloe on the other side of the room. Slow blink. Stare. Chloe, what shall we do?

The room answers without warning or hesitation. The video store. Of course! How long since *Fitzcarraldo*? Maybe he's wondering where she's been. Surely, he'll be there on a Monday night. What an odd day not to work! If he asks about the movie she'll tell him the truth, that she's definitely planning to watch it this week since things have slowed down at her job. Maybe she's even anticipating time for a double feature! She'd better get there quick before the store closes. It's already dark outside and who knows how long it stays open on a weekday. Her standard-issue uniform will have to do for him, and a quick check on hair and makeup. Yes, all presentable. Nothing terribly out of place. The mirror offers its assurances for less than a minute then she rushes down the hall toward the door. Be right back, Chloe!

THE STORE FEELS IRIDESCENT, blinding, a radiant white screen consuming the black of Cora's t-shirt. Her eyes the only movement except the flashing bulbs of the advertisement to the left of the door. The counter, empty. The front of the store, empty. Not how she imagined. What if he hates the job and quit before she could speak to him properly, or let him know in some clever way that he had become the undercurrent of her daily thoughts? He likely gets that all the time from customers but perhaps would rather enjoy hearing it from Cora in particular. Although chances are he'd be put right off. Does it sound creepy, or romantic? Sometimes Cora can't tell. Better keep it quiet for now, just in case.

Just before it all turns to disaster, Cora sees a white button-down peek out from the far corner of the new release wall. Piles of VHS tapes ten to fifteen high surround him at his feet like little worshippers. Disorganized worshippers, to Cora's well-trained eye. No edges are flush, they're all haphazard in tilts and turns. Mathematics itself couldn't sort out the perimeter! Cora's heart beats a little quicker either at the sight of him or the messy stacks, she can't tell which. He reaches down, picks up a video, and looks for its place on the shelf. Magical! They must have been alphabetizing at the exact same time! A cosmic connection held tight by the uppity parallels of H and the meandering grace of S and the fatuous curves of the letter G. Does the alphabet behave the same way toward him? Or does it cut him some slack on account of his height and his voice which its sounds must love to fall into?

Cora needs to find a plan. How would they interact without their compulsory cash register conversation? The shelves give her cover while she waits for inspiration. Browse, peruse, read synopses on the backs of boxes, scoff at some films and smirk at others. Foreign films, *Breathless*, her favorite. Maybe another film will get his attention, but which? Cora has already tried that trick to mixed results.

But which. That's it! Why hadn't she thought of it before? A recommendation. How about asking him for a recommendation? It is his job, after all. Not an odd thing to ask in the slightest! Cora imagines walking across the store, opening with Excuse me, can I ask you a question? Risky, but possibly worth it. He must get questions like that all day long. In fact, maybe he thinks it strange that she *hasn't* asked for a suggestion! He knew about *Fitzcarraldo*, so he likely has a vast repertoire of incredible films that are sure to become Cora's favorite. No doubt! At any rate, he needs to be put to the test, not only for his movie knowledge, but also for his understanding of Cora. What would he think she'd like? It'll be telling, for sure. At this point, how could they move forward without this kind of request? That'd be even riskier! Maybe at the very least Cora will actually get a decent recommendation. Always on the lookout for good cinema. She takes the first step and realizes that two possible outcomes await her: death, or devotion. Does there exist an in between?

He sees her and smiles before she has a chance to use the opening line. Hi. Hi. Blush. Cora must be brave. So, just wondering, since you work here, hope you don't mind if I ask, but are there any movies you commonly recommend, your favorites that someone else, like me, might enjoy? Irritating, the number of words just used! Was that even a sentence? If so, it most certainly could use some editing. Cora's self-critique is interrupted by the sensation of standing next to him, feeling his height, watching his hand hold a movie case fully into his palm, not just with his fingers, like everything in the world can be grasped, nothing is out of reach.

His eyes blink from behind his glasses and wrinkle a little bit as he smiles. Sure, I can probably think of a few you would like, especially if you enjoyed *Fitzcarraldo*. Oh yes, one of my favorites. In that case, yeah, so many come to mind. And just like that, he began, as if he already knows. Let's see. Have you seen any early Polanski? *Early* Polanski? Not sure. I've seen *Rosemary's Baby*. Does that count? Yes, yes it does. Well let's see, what about *Repulsion*? Cora's feet are stuck in the mire and she can't seem to free them. No, I haven't seen that one. Wait, was that the right answer? Maybe she should have lied, said she's seen it least a dozen times, it's kind of a touchstone, hardly separate from her understanding of the world. She could say that and maybe he will see her as she is. But rationally, what if it's a movie that *shouldn't* be a touchstone, of sorts? No, she gave the right answer. The truth will work for the time being. She can always fix it later. Either way, it will likely *become* her favorite. It practically already is!

You haven't seen *Repulsion*? Well, there we have it, then. That's the one you should watch. Beautiful. Perfect. One of my favorites. Technically somewhere between thriller and horror, but truly transcendent of any kind of label. He travels to the next aisle and pulls it from the shelf with his whole hand. Here. And there she is: Catherine Deneuve, staring off in a mildly vacant way, which kind of annoys Cora. Thanks, I'll watch it and let you know what I think. Yes, I'd look forward to that. Cora smiles without him seeing. Triumph!

They make their way to the counter to complete the transaction. Anything else you were looking for tonight? No, just something to watch this week with a bit of free time. He pulls up her account. Unfortunately, I need to remind you that you have two movies out collecting fees at the moment. The fees have gotten to be rather substantial. Oh yes, I know. I'm terrible about returning movies. I promise I'll return this one, though, and the others. Can I still rent or am I banned for life? He smiles. No, not banned. But you will need to pay down some of the fee, which is now just over fifty dollars. Embarrassing. Flushed neck. Fifty dollars? I'm practically a felon! Smiles again. Can I pay twenty-five now and the rest later? Well, generally it needs to be below ten dollars to continue renting, but in this case, since it's so much, I'll make an exception. An exception! It worked. He's making exceptions for Cora already! Clever Cora. She pays, he hands her a receipt. Many thanks. Enjoy the film. I'm sure I will, thank you again! Goodbye! Have a good night! The salutations swirl around Cora as she makes her way toward the door. Success! His favorite is also hers. Her favorite is also his. Two favorites. One Cora. But still, she never got his name!

CORA WAKES TO CHLOE'S pounce. An entire cat body wraps around Cora's foot, hugs tight, and gnaws ravenously on a big toe thankful that it's under a blanket. This, too, Cora's favorite. Her body rises feeling oddly refreshed, reaches down, fluffs Chloe's fur. You really must be hungry this morning! Me too. Let's get up and get some food. Chloe's ritual wake-up call is cut short by Cora's unexpected spring out of bed, her reserves of potential energy bursting to spend itself on the day. It must be the after-effects of last night. Postcard. Movie. Plan to finish the house in plenty of time. It's all coming together, on Cora's own terms!

The Beatle's station calls out to Cora's good mood. Why not drive today? Errands after work will be so much easier, and besides, John and Paul are far preferable to the odors and oily skin she'll likely see on the metro. Energizing drive, or sleepy metro? There's really no question on a day like today.

Ob-La Di, Oh-Bla-Da had been waiting patiently for her to start the car. Perfect. She hums along to words she doesn't know, listens to a few commercials, hums and sings some more. A task list for the day materializes in corners of her euphoria before arriving at work. First, finish the abstract from yesterday. A complicated one about climate change and energy policy, it might last until the afternoon if she can stay focused. Lunch at her desk alone. Then, if it's still available, a hearing on an invasion of Mormon Crickets affecting the

Great Basin area of Utah. Cora can already tell she'll be on the side of the crickets. Why are they called Mormon crickets? Did pioneer Mormons name them that, to put their mark on the world as a cricket's namesake? Or, more delightful to contemplate, perhaps the crickets themselves are Mormon, going about their cricket business while observing the tenets of Joseph Smith's religious vision, chirping out songs of worship in a symphonic cricket chorus.

Julie is waiting for Cora just outside the elevator doors in a state of terrible distress. She throws her arms around Cora's neck with dramatic flair, says It's just so awful. Cora is annoyed but needs to contain her desire to slink out of the embrace. What's so awful? Julie responds, You haven't heard? No, I haven't heard anything. What's going on? Are you okay? Julie forms some half sentences about planes and two buildings in New York, thousands are trapped, no one knows what's going on. Awful, it's just awful. On repeat. Cora is shaken, less by what's been narrated and more by the fact of her good spirits that morning. Isn't it just like the world for this to happen at the exact moment Cora is singing songs and considering the varieties of religious experience for crickets in the Western United States?

244 / SARAH D'STAIR

Everyone in the office listens for updates on NPR while Cora tries to remember what shape the buildings make in the skyline. She wishes she had paid more attention in movies. A few minutes after joining the group, Cora's tummy begins to remind her that coffee is still a necessity. Really, at a time like this? She pads away as quiet as Chloe's stealth to the break room, hoping no one will notice. She thinks about Chloe, hopes she's okay, pours coffee quickly and heads back to the group. Julie puts her hand on Cora's shoulder and Cora allows it. Julie's voice echoes So awful, so awful. A refrain with no variation. Adam looks at Cora from across the room and shrugs as if to say I can't believe what's happening and also to show his dissatisfaction at Julie's histrionics.

The news over the radio narrates to the abstractors and indexers of the congressional indexing service events as they unfold. A second plane has hit the Pentagon, which is only thirty minutes away by car, all of this could become a nationwide event, no one knows. The managers tell everyone to go home, that buildings are being evacuated, the metro will close shortly. Go home right away.

Julie asks if Cora will be alright getting home. Yes, I'll be fine. You should get going before the metro stations close. Julie nods and takes the stairs. Cora needs to pour out her coffee before she leaves but Adam blocks her way. Did you drive today? Yes. Well, have you looked outside at the traffic? No, is it bad? Yeah, it'll take you hours to get home. Oh yeah, that's no good. Adam offers: want to come to my place, watch CNN until the traffic clears? He offers out of kindness, and Cora accepts. Chloe will be okay for a couple more hours. Adam's apartment is just a few blocks away, no need to sit in the car for the entire morning trying to get to great-grandmother's out in the suburbs. They leave work and walk the few blocks chatting about the events of the day.

Adam's living room feels like a light year searching for its own length of time. Light. Immaculate order. Spotless surfaces, bookshelves in perfect order with perfect flush spines. Annoying. At first glance, the books even seem to be organized by genre: environmental nonfiction, political nonfiction, literary fiction, cookbooks and entertainment. John Grisham has his own section, as does Tom Clancy. Had Cora known these facts, she never would have agreed to join him here. A collection of decorative geodes lines the television stand from largest to smallest, a vase of yellow flowers centers the dining table. No dust. Not a spot of grime. Does anyone actually live here? Cora's nerves become undone, split ends that cannot find each other for feeling.

Would you like something to drink? Juice? Orange or apple. Tea? Earl Grey, green, peppermint, honey chamomile. Coffee? Hazelnut or plain. Lemonade? Adam has a number of options for guests. Who has options for guests just lying around in their apartment? This kind of life confuses Cora's more minimalist sensibilities. Just some water will be fine. Cora generally finds a way to avoid complicated decisions.

A beige futon overwhelms Cora with its magazine-cover banality. Not a single thread out of place, no scuffs or tears or dents. She takes a seat, glad to bend the cushions into the shape of her body. Adam turns on the television to images of towers burning and journalists who talk with nothing to say. Julie is right. It truly is awful. So much smoke and debris and tears. Suddenly Cora feels a sense of comfort being here in Adam's strange apartment. She wouldn't feel right in the comfort of great grandmother's house, cozy with Chloe and all the ladies. They wouldn't understand, anyway. It's not a day for them. It's a day for disquiet.

The news images continue, voices continue, Adam's voice

joins the chorus. Guesses at motive. Panic around the country. Grounded flights. Total collapse. Adam critiques the president and the actions of Congress. Cora tells him just today she had planned to write an abstract on a Mormon cricket invasion in Utah. She hopes the fact will illustrate something of her knowledge of Congress but realizes Adam does not see the connection. It occurs to her in that moment that perhaps Adam believes they are dating, that Cora is a girlfriend of some kind, one who takes comfort in his presence during a moment of crisis.

Does he know anything about her recent past with Julie? He can't possibly. Not if he thinks Cora has anything to do with *his* relationship status. No, that near-kiss the other day is telling. He must not know, or care. Cora must admit, there's nothing inherently distasteful about someone other than Julie showing romantic affection. But still, why do either of them care at all? Cora cannot fathom their interest. It's obvious she has nothing to do with them, nothing at all. Can they really mistake her physical presence for engagement, her words for meaning, her laughter for caring at all about what they say? Cora realizes her script is simply too well-written, her improvisational skills lamentably unimpeachable!

After an hour of conversation, Cora asks to investigate the bookshelves. Good little soldiers, Adam's books. They stand at attention, perfectly perpendicular, not a slanted cover in sight. Can they be happy living under such disciplined conditions? Cora needs to find out. She stands and walks over to touch the vibrant blue cover of *The Wealth of Nations*. Next door is a leather-bound edition of Alexis de Tocqueville. Genre and theme take over the alphabet. Fascinating. Her index finger slides down the length of *Democracy in America* as she pushes the volume in just slightly so it's no longer flush with the others. She compliments Adam on his exquisite organizational style, reveals her own penchant for well-ordered lines of shelves.

Adam's body takes a place right behind her as she comments on various titles, even pulls a few down to read the back covers. It's probably time to go home but the books seem to want her to stay. She can't blame them, given the circumstances. She turns and discovers him standing closer than anticipated. He reaches to her face, she feels his mouth close in on hers, feels his hands around her back and neck. It's not so bad, this closeness, he even seems somewhat attractive in such a clean apartment. After a few rather lengthy kisses, he asks if she'd like to go into the bedroom. The news flickers in the background, the windows blind with their light. Cora hears herself say Yes and follows him into a pristine room with actual bedroom furniture, with matching lamps on identical nightstands, precise corners to a bed centered exactly to its square footage. Cora is the antidote to perfection. The room needs her, begs for her hands to pull blankets to the floor and sheets from their tucked corners, the lamp wants to be toppled, the pillows removed from their cases! Here is her reason to stay. She spreads herself on the bed, allows his body to lay alongside, his lips trace the skin of her neck, his hands reach to her face. She grips the blankets and begins to pull as she feels his tongue on the inside of her mouth.

She smears and starts to moan someone wants something from her that she doesn't want to give. Cora can't hold anything against her.

THE WORD 'MULTIPLICATIVE' WOULDN'T leave Cora alone. It followed her outside Adam's apartment, to her car still parked at work, showed itself all along the side of the road, and tucked itself into her purse to be taken inside. Now she's at great-grandmother's, sitting in the wrecked old chair, wondering if the word has a meaning that's not mathematical. Multiplicative. It rolls around the cheeks and the back of the throat, its energy bursts out from the middle syllable and fizzles until it causes a person bite to their own lip. Lovely. The sounds it makes should be its meaning.

Chloe is safe and sound, the house is safe and sound, everything is still in its place. A distinct 'before and after' ushers in the afternoon, a mood almost of depletion. Cora doesn't exactly know what has happened today. She's glad to be with Chloe, with the women on the wall, with the chair and the clothes and the music and the scraps of paper, even with the bratty girl and her raggedy doll. The girl stares at Cora from across the room, accusing and pleading all at once. Pitiable, really. A scared, lost girl. She had made a mistake and someone is angry at her for it. Unjustifiably, perhaps. No wonder she sneers and scoffs. Someone wants something from her that she doesn't want to give. Cora can't hold anything against her for that.

The day has been long for Chloe, who now wants to play after hugs and purrs and a general exchange of the day's emotions. They sit on the floor and pretend a string is the villain. Chloe bats and chases and dives and rolls to attack. She tells Cora when she's done playing by capturing the beast in her mouth and carrying it to the next room out of reach. She finds a nearby water bowl and laps with gusto after such a strenuous affair.

Chloe ends the game just in time for Cora to grow impatient with her body feeling dirty. A bath, that's what she needs. She disregards the fact, for the moment, that she tends to file great-grandmother's bathtub under 'm' for mildly dingy. Cora likes to hide words in drawers where even she cannot find them.

The bath water folds around Cora like an uneasy meditation, a little too hot at first but just fine once relaxed into. So many thoughts beehive Cora's mind, maybe counting slow to five hundred will calm them down. One. Two. Three. Four. Five. Six. At ten Chloe jumps to the ledge of the tub wanting to play bathtub games. Cora scoops some water into her hand, holds it out for Chloe to drink. When the hand bowl empties, Chloe bats at it to say she wants more. Cora refills, Chloe drinks. Eventually Chloe jumps down, chases Cora's hand as it traces along the rim of the tub just peeking out into sight. After a few minutes, she curls up on the bathmat and waits for Cora to be done. Cora and Chloe both doze in each other's company. The room is quiet until the bath water gets cold.

The next morning Susan calls to say the office will be

closed. Very little news of the events had entered great-grand-mother's house. Cora had spent the evening listening to The Beatles on a clock radio and puttering around the house. Not even Judge Sheindlin managed to make his way into the night. Now Cora feels behind, a task list doesn't shrink itself after all. Today needs to be the day. She's kind of glad the office is closed, though would prefer it to be for other reasons. She can't bear to see Julie and Adam, both of them there, one to her left, the other to her right. She'd have no way out. Trapped between two people who have no idea how little she will have to do with them from this day forward.

Cora doesn't feel right ignoring world events just yet. Morning coffee belongs to the news so she takes a walk to the café on the corner a few blocks away. The *New York Times*, a vanilla latte, a pastry of some kind. She'll channel her inner Susan, even have a comment or two to offer around tomorrow's water cooler. The outdoor air will clear the lungs, she'll have a sense that the day actually exists before great-grandmother's door closes behind her.

The latte distracts her from the newspaper as she considers the exact percentage of its superiority to her usual morning coffee. At least fifty percent better. Maybe up to sixty-five.

Just as she questions whether its seventy, an image in the paper catches her eye. She's seen the image before. A man falling. A stark, pale background. A man falling against an empty white frame. A man, falling from the sky. Yesterday. The word 'horrible' slinks in shame at its own incompetency. Cora's thoughts multitask: is there a word grim and terrible enough for such a truth? And where has this image appeared to her before? The answer to the first remains elusive; the answer to the second comes to her during the last few steps of the walk back to the house. Sam Patch, the man who can survive any fall. Tall Tales. Niagara Falls. It's the same image. One a myth, the other dreadful nonfiction. As soon as she walks in the door, *Tall Tales of America*, unearthed from its pile, confirms the similarity. She places the pictures side by side. Both figures so still and quiet and suspended, small bodies against a scene of immense chaos that a still image distorts into peace. Cora cannot comprehend or confront the truth displayed on the floor of great-grandmother's living room. Instinct commits itself to the moment. She tears out the newspaper photo and places it carefully between the book pages, unsure of what else to do or why this course of action is the one

that has chosen her. She closes the cover and, without thinking, places the book on the display case next to the furious
little girl. Cora feels a meaning she cannot access as she turns
away.

There's no question, today needs to be spent getting ahead
on the house. Two weeks will be here quickly and the furniture
removal still hasn't been arranged. A plan finds Cora sitting
inert on the couch. Tomorrow she will call to schedule a pickup of the larger pieces, but not until one of the last days here.
Cora already feels the house groaning under the weight of its
own emptiness, a profound, aching loneliness she knows will
pull her in and crush her. Best to put off that particular inevitability for as long as possible. After that, she'll figure out
what to do with the rest, the boxes and papers and clothes and
bedding and too many other things to contemplate at the moment.

First things first. Before she calls, an inventory must be created, a catalogue list of all items that will be hauled away.
Such an ideal task for today! The list will be long, detailed,
full of specific dimensions and estimated weights, she'll write
in pencil to ensure accuracy, group units by room and size,
leave no object unseen, unheard, unmeasured, unwritten! It

shouldn't take all that long, and maybe she'll have time to watch *Repulsion* as a prize for her diligence. She'll deserve a treat by then. After all, the house will practically be done.

Chloe, let's get some music going to help us out. Something peppy, yes? Something to put a spring in our steps. People are sad and the house is sad but we can cheer them up, don't you think? Cora finds the only record that she hasn't yet played, the nineteen fifty-nine Barbershop Chorus winners recorded live at the Chicago Opera House. What a well-groomed collection of men on the cover! Yes, this will do. Cora sets the needle and turns her attention to pencil and paper. A clean notebook makes itself available to her, but a writing utensil proves a bit more obscure. Nothing in her purse, nothing on the kitchen counter or living room table. Chloe, where did you hide all the pencils? She opens a drawer near the phone hanging on the kitchen wall. Proverbial junk! Where did this drawer come from? Decks of playing cards, paper clips, broken flashlight, empty checkbook covers, two spoons, pens and dry markers, loose buttons, thumbtacks, masking tape, old eyeglasses, coins and a few two-dollar bills, magnifying glass, bookmarks, loose nails and screws. Cora can see nothing to save in this drawer, except the two pencils that seem to be in working order. There is still so much left to do. Who are we kidding, Chloe? Maybe we can get rid of every last thing in this entire house, haul it all away in one majestic display of power. At least it all could stay together, the dolls would still have each other, the naked ladies could marvel at each other on the way to the furnace, no one would ever be separated again!

It will never happen. Cora won't let it. Somehow, we will make this alright, Chloe. But for now, onward! Living room: sofa, lounge chair, decorative table, coffee table, side table, television with stand. Dining room: small round table and four chairs. The box with Chloe's broken glass still lingers on the floor. That will need to be thrown out, eventually. Perhaps the hundreds of dishes on the kitchen counter can be boxed and removed with the furniture. In parenthesis: (dishes?). First bedroom: double bed, nightstand, bookshelf, small chair. Second bedroom: queen bed, large dresser, two nightstands, lounge chair, chest of drawers. Third bedroom: desk, two bookshelves. Dimensions will come later, but this is a good start. Cora's list has become the end point of accumulation, and there is still so much to be added! Great-grandmother's rings and bracelets, necklaces, brushes, jackets, sweaters, records, books, pictures, postcards, catalogues, and chairs. Thousands and thousands of items are left off Cora's list even though they have just as much right to be there. They exist, do they not? And must be regarded, chosen or not chosen, pardoned or destroyed. Cora once again boards a train headed for the wrong station. Remember the purpose of the list! Just the large items, Cora. It's no slight against the others! An adolescent word problem creeps between the lines on Cora's notebook paper. Great-grandmother has left x number of objects with y mass and z volume. The cumulative values of x, y, z equal the retrospective inverse of great-grandmother's existential meaning. Solve. Cora makes some preliminary calculations in the margins of her paper, but then remembers that she has not yet inventoried the sunroom. In fact, she has avoided it at all cost for nearly a year.

The sunroom door opens to a vast and faded assembly of large furniture items, wood-stained and haphazard, a room as boring as infinity. A few times, Cora ventured out to assess the labor that would be involved, but quickly retreated. The pieces are in general too large for her to move by herself, yet someone had been disrespectful enough to position them in slants and clusters with no discernable organizational pattern. It's too much. Nothing to be done. Yet now, Cora needs to make a list. She opens the door attached to the kitchen and steps one foot inside. Unfathomable. Where did it all come from? Were these items displaced when great-grandmother bought new furniture? Did she intend to keep them here forever? Were they unwanted gifts? Antique store impulse purchases? Or stored here from someone else's overcrowded life? Cora can't help but feel a little sorry for not paying more attention sooner. What did they ever do to deserve such neglect? Such disuse, disintegration, disarray, decay, with no shielding from the harsh light, no temperature control whatsoever!

Suffocating. Stuffy. Hot. The room sucks the words right out of Cora's throat. The place definitely needs some air. She opens the back door out to the overgrown yard, which Cora assumes is full of snakes and giant insects and other wildlife she would not like to encounter. A slight breeze flows in and out of the wreckage through the screen door. At least it's bearable enough to write down the names of things. Two large, sun-stained dressers. A windowed hutch still with dust stains where figurines and other knick-knackery once stood. A large, unopened trunk that Cora knows she needs to open at some point. A side table holding a glorious set of five rotary phones all from different eras. Cora fingers the circular dial on one of them and pretends to call a number. Two empty magazine racks. A massive tabletop television with a twenty-channel dial. An oversized spinning globe. Two heavy wooden headboards leaned to the wall and three multi-stained mattresses. A tall, complicated secretary desk with delicious secret drawers and cubbies.

Cora's long list stares back at her in triumph. Even if they do nothing else today, they will call it a success. Tomorrow, a quick phone call will arrange for all of this to be picked up, taken away to who knows where but that can't be her concern. It needs to be done. The grandparents are counting on her and she and Chloe really can't stay here forever anyway. If only it were more clear the precise day she needs to move out, then she could schedule the pickup for just the day before. The entire house, empty and alone just as she promised. Not a box or paper or utensil left to be seen. Even she and Chloe will be gone, maybe spending the night in a fancy hotel!

The unopened trunk and all the little drawers need to be opened and, if necessary, sorted. But that can be done later. Right now, Cora is thirsty. Her throat is full of hot dust. She'll return to the sunroom later to finish organizing, perhaps if the kitchen door is left open a nice breezy current will clear out the foul taste in the air. As she makes her way into the kitchen for a glass of water, Cora's eye catches a small piece of paper: "Now we behold the embers flee...." She is reminded without question that words have an insidious way of changing their meanings behind a person's back.

The sunroom will be completely finished by the end of the evening, most definitely, but while it's being freed of its foul humor, the day needs to continue on its utilitarian streak. No moment wasted, not today! Now that the furniture is properly accounted for, perhaps great-grandmother's bedroom could use another look. The endless piles of jewelry need to be appraised, but that won't take long. She'll gather it up and take it to a place she knows this weekend. But the clothes. That's another matter. Some may be in good enough shape to be sold second hand, some simply need to be sent to the fire. It's a good day for sorting, so let's begin there, shall we, Chloe? Three piles: sell, donate, discard. Great-grandmother's bedroom is almost as musty as the sunroom so Cora opens a window to let in some air.

The piles of clothing have preserved their geometric designs with immaculate care. Impressive! A good sorting begins to reveal that great-grandmother was actually quite stylish at one time, at least from a retro-vintage standpoint. Most of the clothes clearly originated in the sixties, bright colors, slim silhouettes, fitted skirt suits and wool pants. A tad too big for Cora's slight frame, but then again, Cora wonders. How would she look in sixties chic, or as a nineteen-fifties workaday woman? There's no harm in trying a thing or two on. In fact, it'd be a shame to send these lovely items off without a final appreciation.

Cora sheds her house pants and t-shirt in favor of a dark blue tweed skirt and yellow blouse, block style blazer, silk scarf. Despite the outfit's slightly oversized aesthetic, Cora looks remarkably similar to a young Catherine Deneuve, or a girl right out of French New Wave dancing in a café in Paris. Cora admits she looks cute and wishes she had the confidence to wear such an ensemble in public. However, the fabric is exceedingly uncomfortable, itchy and parched, likely full of dust mites or other creepy crawlies. She walks out to the living room to show Chloe. Chloe, what do you think? Should I wear this to the video store next time I go? He'd find me irresistible!

Chloe looks up from her spot next to the dolls and gives Cora a nod of approval.

Great-grandmother's chair puts Cora within petting distance of Chloe. She sits, the wooly fabric scratching the skin of her thighs, but no sacrifice is too great for a moment of affection. What a strange little scene, silent except the turntable spinning at the record's end. No music. No cars outside. No birds twittering. Chloe isn't even purring, though she's perfectly happy. The newspaper lay unread on the coffee table but it, too, keeps quiet. Cora thinks of Julie in an unexpected wave of empathy. How would she feel if she learned about the events of yesterday with Adam? Sad. Hurt. Confused. Maybe jealous. Why didn't Cora think of that sooner? What's keeping her from telling Julie the truth, that Cora is simply unavailable for any kind of emotional connection? That she's unfit? Unable? Untenable? No, the reasonable thing never occurs to Cora until it's too late. And now look at what a mess she's made. No excuse would be clever enough to put things back in order. Maybe the office will stay closed all week. If not, she can call out. Tell Susan about great-grandmother's house, the imminent deadline. Except nothing will work. Julie would call. Adam would call. Everyone would call and leave messages Cora would not want to hear and would not want to answer. Regardless of her course of action at this point, Cora will end up hurting these rather nice people through no fault of her own. It's a dilemma. A complex hearing to abstract, too many experts, too many politicians, too many words Cora doesn't understand!

Cora lingers in the living room until her legs are rabid with irritation. Chloe, your cuteness is keeping my legs in a fit of rage. I need to stop petting you now. It's time to take off this skirt before another rash carpe diems all over my lower half. Cora feels full of dusty bugs and bits of tweedy strings. The itchy skirt comes off before she reaches the bedroom, then the scarf and blouse. Her house clothes panic at the thought of her dirty skin. Okay, a shower first, then. It's the right thing to do, but then, no more delays. Back to work!

A sandwich bag dutifully waits to be stuffed with more of Cora's hair. The collection is getting quite substantial, maybe even enough for a larger bag, a gallon bag! Science serves Cora well in its principles of data analysis. There's no doubt: great-grandmother's house is slowly re-positioning Cora's body in space, a bit here, a bit there, this bit in a cup, that bit in a bag. Luckily Cora has the good sense to keep it all to-gether on the bathroom counter. Oh well, only two more weeks. At this rate, it would take years to disperse the totality of Cora and the house simply doesn't have that kind of time.

In the absence of a vexing abstract to work out in the shower, Cora decides to work out her life. Time to sort it all into piles and decide what to do with them. First, her living situation. Find an apartment closer to work, maybe even within walking distance. That will save on transportation costs, allow her to sleep a little later, and perhaps even help her feel more connected to the people who populate her days. Next, Julie. And Adam. They belong in the same pile. She will tell them both the truth. Or her version of the truth. She needs some time to sort herself out after this ordeal with great-grand-mother's house and finding a new place to live. How can they argue with that logic? Added bonus: their feelings will be saved since they will learn nothing of the overlapping associ-ations. If they find out amongst each other, Cora will simply apologize and tell them the fluctuation in life circumstances caused her to make poor decisions. Maybe they'll want noth-ing to do with her after that. And isn't that an indicator of true success? And Theresa: her pile has already been whisked away to the furnace. Done, and done. All in all, things are working out rather well and even looking up. And think of it, tomorrow she'll get to spend her day in peace with Mormon crickets!

Chloe isn't on the mat when Cora gets out of the shower. What a day for Chloe to decide to go rogue! Sometimes she prefers nibbling on food or finding a ray of sunlight to sitting with Cora in the steamy bathroom. It makes sense. Cora dries herself off, dresses in appeased house clothes, and makes her way to the living room to see if Chloe is still on the sofa. Chloe does get comfortable when she's with those dolls.

No luck. Chloe's not on the couch. She's not near her food or on the dining room table. Chloe, where have you gone, silly girl? Bathroom again. No Chloe. Third bedroom with all the books and papers. Closet, great-grandmother's room with the clothes. Cora's bedroom, under the bed, under the blankets, in the closet. Bathroom again. Living room, under the couch, under the table, behind the record albums. Kitchen, inside cupboards, half-open boxes, hallway, under towels and envelopes, third bedroom again, closets again, under the beds again. No Chloe anywhere. The sunroom. It's warm in there and maybe Chloe wanted to explore. Maybe she's lounging on a piece of furniture soaking up rays. It'd be a perfect place for her, yes, of course. Cora had left the door open in the kitchen, she's sure to be there. Chloe, are you in here? Where did you go? Cora checks every surface, each bit of open carpet. Under the furniture, behind the headboards and magazine racks, in the drawers of the hutch just in case. Chloe, where are you? Kiss, kiss, Chloe. Kiss kiss, Chloe. Chloe, where you are, my girl? Where are you hiding? Kitchen again. Cora shakes Chloe's bag of dry food. Are you hungry, my Chloe? No sound, no movement, only stillness and quiet. Chloe? Have you found someplace silly in this silly house to hide? Kiss kiss, Chloe? Chloe? Living room again. Bedrooms again. Closets again. Under the sofa. Behind the dolls.

Worry sets in but not yet panic. She just got a clean bill of health and has seemed fit and fine so she can't be laying sick somewhere. She's never hidden from Cora before. Had she gotten outside somehow? But how? Cora checks the doors and windows, makes sure the open window in great-grand-mother's bedroom is secure. The sunroom? Cora puts pressure on every dingy window lining the walls. Everything seems to be shut tight. She looks out to the backyard through the worn screen door. She traces her hand around the screen to see if any part is loose. By the time her hand reaches the bottom of the screen, all the answers in the universe come tumbling down like bricks onto her sun-soaked head. The screen is loose at the bottom, a rather large opening out to the mangy backyard if a cat were to investigate with her little nose or paws. Chloe must have been exploring, must have seen a squirrel or bird, must have put just enough pressure on the screen to find a way into the out of doors!

Cora wants to call the backyard grizzly but also doesn't want to cause it any offence. Not with her Chloe out here! She walks the perimeter near the obscured chain link fence, peeks as much as she can into the thick bushes and weeds. Chloe, are you out here? She searches on the side of the house and out in front, near the garage entrance, on the sidewalk and down the road. Back of the house again, a peek into the neighbors backyards on both sides. Chloe? Where are you, my girl? Cora wanders around the house until the evening. Walks the length of the neighborhood. Knocks on every person's door for two blocks in each direction. Have you seen a calico tabby, a little overweight, friendly but maybe a little skittish? Her name is Chloe. Here is my phone number, if you see her, please call!

The evening has almost turned to darkness and still no sign of Chloe. Maybe she went back inside the house. Cora enters through the sunroom door and checks all over once again, the kitchen, the sofa, the bedrooms, the sunroom again. She turns on all the lights in the house, the outdoor lights, too, and rips away the loosened screen so Chloe can get back inside with ease. She calls for Chloe. She calls and calls and calls and calls. She calls from the back steps, kiss kiss, call call, until the night is very dark. A few cars drive by, a streetlamp clicks awake. A cool breeze brushes her bare arms but Cora doesn't notice. She calls and calls and calls. Chloe? Chloe! But Chloe is nowhere to be found.

What should Cora do? She can't go to bed, can't eat any dinner, can't listen to music or work in the house. The back steps and a bowl of Chloe's favorite food keep her company until two in the morning. Chloe? Can you hear me, Chloe? Can you hear me, my girl? Cora searches in the dark for two night-glinted eyes but can't find them. Searches in the blackness under cars in driveways and on the street, under trees and between overgrown bushes. No eyes, no Chloe. She can't just leave Chloe alone outside. Chloe's never lived outside before. How shall she find her way? Stay safe from other animals? Other people? Will she call out for help if she needs it? What if some unthinking little girl finds her and Chloe is nice and the girl takes her home and keeps her captive? Chloe is micro-chipped, but do they have Cora's current information? She'll need to call around tomorrow to all the local veterinarians and animal shelters just in case. At two in the morning, there is nothing for Cora to do. She can only call and call and call and hope Chloe returns. Chloe will know the way. She will know the way back to Cora.

Facts must be faced. Eventually, Cora will be too tired to sit on the steps in the backyard and will need to sleep. Better get prepared for this unfortunate inevitability. She makes her way to their bedroom and sees Chloe's empty blanket bed. It's the first time tonight her eyes decide to cry. She can't sleep with-out Chloe. Can Chloe sleep without her? A decision must be made so Cora makes it. She removes all the blankets from the bed and carries them to the sunroom. She needs every blanket in the house. All of them gather together, even the ones on great-grandmother's bed, all together in a pile on the floor. She finds a spot just big enough for her body to lay them all flat on the ragged carpet. A city of silent furniture rises around her as she fashions a bed even Chloe would find comfortable. She'll sit here with the door open all night. Mosquitos and gnats already begin to surround her but she doesn't care. If

Chloe sleeps with the bugs tonight, then so does Cora. Maybe if she stays here long enough, Chloe will come back during the night. Maybe she'll wake up to Chloe sleeping on the little blanket bed Cora has transported here intact. Maybe Chloe will get hungry and find her way to her morsels and gravy. She'll need to come back at some point, won't she? To find food if nothing else?

The kitchen light hardly pierces the darkness that surrounds Cora on her new bed in the sunroom. Outside, a black night echoes out Chloe, Chloe, Chloe without Cora needing to say it. It knows Chloe's name by heart. The silence is lonely but Cora needs to hear if the slightest mew cries out to her. She sits in the dark for hours. Quiet. Alone. Afraid. As the sun almost rises, her body finally gives up and dozes without her permission. It's a good thing it fell asleep in secret. She'd be furious if she knew!

The hot sun sends in panic to wake Cora with a start. It's been several hours and all she's done is sleep! She looks all around. Chloe's bed, empty. The sunroom, empty. She searches the house again. Empty. Chloe's food dish, empty. Probably the squirrels. Cora loves squirrels but doesn't want them to eat Chloe's food. She refills the bowl with morsels and gravy, refills the water, checks again outside in the light. Chloe? Chloe! Chloe, can you hear me? Chloe! Chloe! Chloe? She walks outside all day, checks the house, all day. She calls in sick to work. Sketches out posters to hang on mailboxes and doors. She naps in the sunroom. She searches again. She calls and calls and calls and calls.

PART SEVEN

PART SEVEN

THE SUNROOM CRADLES CORA in its dirty arms, rocks her to sleep and sings her a lullaby, strokes her hair to the melody of a love song no one understands. Its windows flood her face with sunlight, bring to life the hot sweat and dust that festers on her skin. Remnants of grief laze about her blanket bed, candy wrappers and empty cans of soda, half-eaten pizzas still in their boxes, a painting, taken from the living room, of a nude goddess whose face is full of peace, dozens of books thrown at random on the floor. No Chloe, though. The screen door, still open, serenades Cora with the conversational twitter of backyard birds, breezes though gnarled shrubs and tall weeds, the occasional hum of a passing car. Mostly, Cora hears the continuous drone of the television set, relocated from the living room and plugged into the kitchen wall, cord outstretched to meet Cora in the bed that has become her home.

A dusty VCR whirls and hisses out sounds from *Fitzcarraldo* all day and all night, except at eleven-thirty when Judge Sheindlin comes to visit. Cora has made friends with the sunroom because it is where Chloe will return. She will keep vigil until then, curled against its tender breast, measuring time to the beat of its heart. Beat. One minute. Beat. Two minutes. Beat. Three minutes. Beat. Four minutes. Beat. Five minutes more without Chloe. A beautiful lunatic heaves a ship across a mountain, a faithful man dies at his hand, a forest swallows the sound of Caruso. Cora slips down into the dark river in the night misted with fog.

Minutes had passed for three days. Some minutes had roamed the neighborhood with photocopied signs made with markers and hung with tape. Others called in sick to work. A few each day made telephone calls to animal shelters and hospitals, and a good number spent themselves around nearby parts of town just in case Chloe wandered further than one would expect. Some made sure to put out new food and water all day even though Chloe never ate it. The minutes had persevered without hesitation and had done everything they could think to do. Despite their efforts to bring Chloe home, they really couldn't blame her for leaving. Cora *had* been spending an excessive amount of time outside the house for no good reason. Remember how she'd spent that time with Julie, out to her house, out to Adam's and to the golf course and who knows why? Remember how she spends every weekday amused and immersed in some random senator's words? And laughing now and then at the absurdity she finds stamped on pages with solid black ink? All while Chloe waits for her at the front door? Chloe deserves a vacation from the monotony of life with Cora. She must have been desperate for an adventure with the birds and mice and butterflies and the taste of grass on her tongue!

If only the air conditioning would work a little harder to make it out to the sunroom. But Cora can't complain. No one is there to see her in ragged shorts and an old, torn t-shirt. No one can see her unbrushed teeth, smell her unwashed hair, judge her for being braless in broad daylight. Not that they aren't trying. So far, they've only gotten as close as the answering machine allows them, but who's to say what will happen in the coming days? Adam and Julie say they are worried. Susan wonders when she'll be back at work. And worst of all, the grandparents have announced they will be arriving a few days ahead of schedule. They also want an update on the house. All these voices speak only when Cora presses Play. They come to her from an undiscovered universe, similar to ours in height, but not in weight.

Books from great-grandmother's shelves pride themselves on keeping Cora occupied. They have taught her all about fish populations in North America, best practices in collecting rare marbles, and how to crochet a sweater using Irish wool. At present the historical fiction of Louise Mühlbach struggles to hold her attention. She grasps the dark green hardback in her whole hand, an echo of a memory from a lifetime ago. Only the most mournful of the five she found on the shelf had gotten her attention, the story of a Prussian queen who tries to convince Napoleon not to invade. The novel opens with a Viennese population "paralyzed with terror" so that even the "stoutest hearts seemed broken." The stoutest hearts. The phrase belongs on the living room wall or the hallway with the others but Cora has no energy to write it down and hang it. The rest of the prose proves itself flat, hardly concerned with language at all, a relief to Cora so she can put aside her guilt at giving the book only a glimpse of her attention. An odd sensation wraps around Cora in the sunroom, something vaguely similar to a VHS tape that won't rewind, or the blue light of the television just before it dims to black.

Sinister clouds consume the backyard as suddenly as Cora stands from her bed. Rain, a summer afternoon deluge. Chloe will get wet and chilled. Chloe, do you know I am here where it's safe and dry? Cora peers out the screen door but sees no sign or trace. Nothing to do except perhaps find a drink of water to satisfy hours of thirst. Cora threads herself around the television cord to her make way into the kitchen, rinses out the lobster mug and fills it from the tap. Can she sit in the dining room for a few minutes? Cora takes her seat in a sparkling yellow chair just to test the theory. She sees the numerous bowls and cups of water carefully placed all around for Chloe. Discomfort. Disquiet. An image of Glenn Gould takes shape in her imagination. Forty-five seconds and a chair, a short film from a movie she loves. Or used to love. She can't tell what she loves anymore. Can Cora sit very still in a chair? Sense time in a space other than a room made of windows? Has she been inventing their love all along? The kisses and pets, the games and pounces and purrs? A crisis of faith nestles into the crook of Cora's neck where Chloe used to lay. It wraps its tail around her throat and bites her on the cheek.

One of great-grandmother's drinking glasses, layered with fine dust, stares at Cora from the dining room table and reminds her that she had forbidden Chloe from knocking it down. An act of love? Or selfishness? What would have been the harm? It would have been an easy mess to clear. How often does Cora steal Chloe's joy? With absence, with putting an end to play sessions before she's ready to stop, with serving her favorite food only on special occasions? Cora removes the barricade she engineered to keep the glasses safe. Chloe, if you come back, you can knock down every glass in the world. Promise! All the joy will be yours no matter what! Cora wonders what the glasses would say about that but decides she really doesn't care. What would it feel like to knock one over, to push a paw to its side, anticipate the slow scoot to the edge, to watch it fall and splinter on the floor? Nothing is stopping Cora anymore. She can do it if she wants. On Chloe's behalf, or on her own. Or both together.

She taps a fingertip to the one with the picture of Yosemite Sam on the front, the one she drank from as a child even though she never liked the way Yosemite Sam burst through saloon doors brandishing his guns. How does Chloe do it? Tap, tap, tap. Tap, tap. Closer and closer to the edge, closer still, closer, closer, then swat, over the edge it falls, slow motion to the hard ground in a grand, celebratory crash. Would the next one feel the same? Let's try the Tasmanian Devil. She never liked him much either. Tap, tap, tap. Cora will investigate how it feels to be Chloe. Tap, tap. Tap. Over the edge and down, down, crash, like the wild west of broken glass. And what about another? Petunia Pig, how will you feel? And Tweety? Wile E. Coyote? What about Daffy Duck? How does it feel to smash Daffy to a hundred pieces on great-grandmother's linoleum floor? After the characters have gone, only flower prints and transparent glassware remain. No matter. No one could stop her now. Cora spreads the length of her arm out on the table, tap, tap, tap to them all, all at once, all that are left will join the riotous ensemble as supporting characters, a Greek chorus of shards and flecks disseminating their wisdom to the crowd.

Cora has no time to ruminate on the beauty of her workmanship, her efficiency, her skill in keeping it all between the margins. Chloe could be walking through the door at this very moment! She'd be hungry and would shuffle through the kitchen on the way to where her food bowl usually sits. And what would she find? A paw full of cuts and splinters! Cora needs to act fast. Shoes would be a reasonable start but Cora is surrounded by broken glass. A quick, hopeful hop to the living room carpet, a 'whew' of relief, and a pair of patient flip flops ready her for the job ahead. She sweeps the entire throng into the dustbin, every last bit she can find, and wishes she were a creator of the mosaic arts so they could be properly displayed in all their intricate tessellations. Instead, her efforts are mixed in the corner box with Chloe's, the box she had meant to take out to the trash. No more glasses for drinking. No more Looney Tunes. Now they lounge in cardboard as powerless as lower-case letters, a fricassee of joy and sadness, a mournful lost holding of paw and hand.

After Cora mops the floor and tests the area with her bare feet, she installs herself again in the sunroom to wait for Chloe. *Fitzcarraldo*, Louise of Prussia, snacks and rotting pizza. A backyard check, a repetition of name. A darkening sky. A fluffing of blankets. Cora is tired but cannot sleep. *The People's Court* entertains her for half an hour but then loneliness sneaks into her bed. If only she could wait in the living room with all the eyes, the dolls, the girl, the women. The goddess in the painting looks into the distant corner of the sunroom while Cora attempts to find a resolution. The dolls. They could be some company, at least. Though the guilt stings with each step, she chooses two from the sofa to join her in the waiting room. The small one with pretty eyes that open and close, the dirty one with one eye closed. Purgatory now has a population of four. Five if you count the desperate queen whose words lay open next to the pillow. Evening comes to an end. Chloe can find her food and water, the outside light is on, murmurs from the television coalesce with an acapella of crickets.

CORA WAKES WITH AN uneasy feeling, perhaps because she knows she slept through the night. Day four. Morning news, sunshine, two dolls and dirt and grime. Time for coffee and the routine search for Chloe. Food bowl outside: empty again. Refill. Refill water. Chloe! Chloe? Peer in the bushes and all around the fence, scan the perimeter of the house and the neighbor's yards. Look under trees and cars and shrubs. She could be scared, hiding anywhere in all this mess. She must hear Cora calling her name. Where could she be?

Over a lobster cup of coffee Cora's skin and hair remind her that she hasn't showered since the moment of Chloe's disappearance. Could the shower be to blame? Cora's habit of staying in the water for twenty minutes too long every day? If she showers today, would the curse be broken? Would clean skin bring Chloe home? Either way, it's day four and it is time to shower and perhaps even leave the house on some make-believe errand just to test it out. Maybe day four will be the last. I promise, Chloe. Just a quick shower. A quick jaunt to the store. Before she walks to the back of the house, Cora places the two dolls back in their spots on the couch. No need to leave them in the sad, hot sunroom.

The bathroom mirror finds Cora to be a disgrace. Slumped shoulders, drooping eyes, dirty black t-shirt. Even her brilliant experiment testing the degradation of hair has failed to find completion. Her hair could be scattered anywhere by now: the sunroom, the backyard, all across the neighborhood. No point in collecting. The mirror feels ridiculous surrounded by her body's remainders, a collage of suffering skin and nail. Pathetic. Cora can hardly bring herself to look at the eyes in the mirror, a judge and jury of two, ready to condemn criminal and victim both in equal measure.

The shower helps, Cora must admit. Her body feels refreshed; a minimal appearance of civility prepares her in case the world would force an encounter. Her uniform, jeans and black t-shirt, carry traces of Chloe everywhere Cora goes, fur that clings to threads of fabric despite efforts to lint roll or wash them away. Regret and confusion walk down the hall with Cora. These gold and white bits of Chloe holding on to her clothing, how could she ever have wished them away?

Somewhere deep within the connective tissue that surrounds Cora's mind exists the belief that one must not simply come to a halt. A watched pot never boils, after all. Her idea about the shower was a step in the right direction. But now what? The silence is punctuated only by faint undertones from the sunroom of television news, towers and fires and counting the dead. Such an obsession with numbers can't help her now, or anyone for that matter, or Chloe. *Fitzcarraldo* playing softly is the only sound she can bear, the whispers, the depraved lunatic, the trees and the water. Her eyes involuntarily search for Chloe in all the usual spots on the way through the living room and kitchen, involuntarily absorb the colors hung on the walls and scattered on the floor, rest for a half second on a scrap of paper inscribed with a snippet of poetry. "These are my starry solitudes." She tries to catch an incipient tear but fails. Starry solitudes, beautiful and meaningless without referent, a living consciousness unwilling to give her respite from understanding. As she presses play on the video cassette recorder, a melancholy silence begins another cycle of repetition. Quiet, then sound. Quiet, then sound. Quiet. Sound. Quiet. Sound. No escape. The pattern is set. These are my starry solitudes.

The blanket bed grows softer every day despite Cora's protestations. And her worry. The house cannot be allowed to swallow her up! Some attempt must be made to break free. This morning's shower was an excellent start, but what can be done for the rest of the day? Can she bring herself to leave the house? It may not be possible, only one way to find out. First, a quick roam around the neighborhood will serve as both a test run and another attempt to find Chloe. Maybe she'll end up at the coffee shop, and wouldn't that be an achievement? Of course the sunroom door needs to be left open, but the screen can shut itself all it wants. No love lost for the screen door. Cora steps outside to begin today's session. Chloe! Chloe? Chloe, you must be somewhere. Where are you, my Chloe? Chloe! Chloooooeeeee.

By now Cora is used to returning home empty-handed.

There must be a way to leave the house. If she can wander the streets, why can't she find a destination a bit further out, if for no other reason than to remind her body that someplace else exists? Even the sunroom goads her to leave by this point, tells her it's okay, Chloe will wait here for you if she returns. She'll walk right through on the way to the sofa and she'll sleep with the dolls and she'll watch for you at the door. Alright. Cora considers both sides of the debate before she stands to look for her shoes. I suppose you're right. I should go, just for a few minutes. Maybe to the video store. It's been a while and somehow the thought is comforting. A quick browse around, check out the new releases, make sure he hasn't also disappeared.

Her car pulls into the parking lot just in time to see him opening the front door for the day's business. White button-down. Tall. He seems to know Cora has arrived. She waits a moment before stepping out of the car just to avoid any awkwardness. Let him get settled first, it's the least she could do. By the time she enters the store he has already taken a spot at the counter, laptop open, typing away. Is he typing just to avoid her? Didn't he know she was about to walk through the door? Cora isn't sure whether or not to feel slighted. At least he gives her a smile and a nod as she makes her way to the farthest new release wall.

The store feels quiet and empty and lost. All the movies seem untitled despite words printed on their covers. Patterns and colors do their best to make sense but their audience is unwilling. At least Cora is used to bright light after spending so many days in the sunroom. The sunroom. Chloe. So far away. Chloe, are you walking through the screen door this very minute, at the precise second you'd feel most abandoned? Cora is outside the house in body but not in mind.

Before she knows what's happening, the video store clerk appears just next to where Cora stands to place some movies along the wall. Are they the only two people in the store? How hidden are their mutual wishes! His hands reach toward a tall shelf but his eyes look over at Cora. He asks with a casual air, How did you like *Repulsion*? The question is not a surprise at all but must he always ask only about movies she hasn't seen? Oh, it's now one of my favorite things in the world, thank you for the introduction! She continues to look at him while his voice fills the empty space. Speaking of introductions, and Polanski, my name is Roman. Is also Roman, like Polanski though I'm not named after him, I don't think. Cora remembers one must control oneself in these kinds of situations. Control. Do not say what is on your mind! In French his name is novel. Novel, of all things! Cora responds with a handshake, out of nowhere! Very nice to meet you, Roman, my name is Chloe. Wait, did I say Chloe? No. I mean Cora. My name is Cora, not Chloe, but you must already know that from my secret FBI rental file. Sorry, I really do know my name. Nervous laugh. He needs no explanation but she offers one anyway. My cat's name is Chloe, I don't know why I said that. Nod. Beat. A thought finds her helpless in a video store. Maybe she should be honest for just a few minutes? What could be the harm? On the spot decisions seldom work for her, but okay, here goes! Actually. Inhale. I do know why I said that. It's just, she's been on my mind. She disappeared a few days ago. Four days ago. I've been going a little crazy without her. He asks, How did she get lost? The truth wraps itself around her words once again. Oh, well, I didn't realize the screen was loose on the door to the backyard. She must have gotten out that way. It's all I can figure. But I don't understand where she could have gone. I've been looking all over and she hasn't come back even once. So yeah, a little crazy. A little lost without her. He tells her, Try not to worry. He's had a good number of cats in his life, indoor and outdoor, and they have always come back. That's his experience, anyway. They just like adventure sometimes. Half smile. Yes, I hope so.

Silence. He places a movie on a shelf. She pulls one off to look. After one more new release finds its place in the alphabet, he turns and looks at Cora. She looks right back and does not look away. He inhales. She exhales. She hears his deep voice say the words, You know what? Beat. Let's go look. Simple. A few simple words. A statement, not a question. Let's go look? What do you mean? Cora doesn't understand. Let's go look for her. I'll help you. Pause. You want to help me look for my lost cat? Slight head shake, confusion. Yes, I do. Let's go look. But aren't you working? Yeah, but my co-worker is in the back. He can cover the next couple of hours. It's no problem. Let's just go look. So easy. Three words versus the whole of his other life! Hold on, I'll be right back. Cora holds on. He goes into the door in the far back of the store and then returns to the front counter, places his laptop in its bag, and gestures for her to follow him as he walks out the door. Let's go look, he had said. Several times. Cora says, Okay.

Yes, let's go look. Cora realizes her eyes have welled with tears.

The drive to great-grandmother's house with Roman resembles the interior structure of an abstract. Phrases in ideal succession, subjects and predicates uncluttered, balanced like sophisticated equations. Their conversation stays flush within the margin, fills the blank page with the gift of distraction. Roman asks about Chloe, how long they had been together, her personality, how she likes to play. Over "Don't Let Me Down" she learns that he also listens to The Beatles station, and they question in unison how long such a station can last. The sun shines hot on Cora's arm and she feels the heat on her skin. Just around the corner from the house, he points out a park where he used to play as a child. Cora remembers playing in the same park on family visits and says so. They both wonder if they ever played there together.

When they arrive at great-grandmother's, they get out of the car and go immediately to the back of the house. Roman and Cora peer into the foliage and weeds that are exhausted from hearing Chloe's name. Cora calls out for her over and over while Roman stays quiet. No Chloe. Cora says she's not surprised. She's just, gone. They walk around the front of the

house, the neighborhood streets, Roman sneaks into other people's backyards on Cora's behalf. They begin to talk. They
talk and talk and talk. Movies. Books. Growing up with TV as
babysitter and Saturday morning cartoons and endless bowls
of cereal. Wes Anderson, *Bottle Rocket* for over an hour, the
trailer for *The Royal Tenenbaums* and plans to see it together
maybe when it comes out. Roman Polanski and his name and
her name and the novels of Dostoyevsky and memorized bits
of T.S. Eliot. The genius of Edward Albee and *Who's Afraid
of Virginia Woolf* and George and Martha as the most beautiful love story they've ever seen. And speaking of Virginia
Woolf, *To the Lighthouse* has a marvelously perfect title but
neither of them has ever been able to finish the novel to the
end. Jean-Luc Godard and the café dance scene in *Band of
Outsiders* and Jim Jarmusch and the walking down the street
scene in *Stranger than Paradise* and how nineteen eighty-four
was probably one of the best years for American cinema. Old
television shows they loved to watch as kids like *Who's the
Boss* and their mutual infatuation with Mr. Belvedere and his
diary. They talk about all the things Cora loves but had never
realized how much, and all the things Cora wants to love because if he loves them she knows she will love them too. They

sometimes walk without talking for a few steps and then one of them will talk again. They look for Chloe and call her name. They talk some more. They agree and disagree and even Cora finds a way to laugh because Roman makes the world too delightful for her to bear.

Eventually they circle back to the house and sit on the back steps to talk some more. Cora tells Roman all about her current predicament: great-grandmother's death, her task for the past year, the packing and the deadlines, the hidden treasures, the organizational strategies she recognizes are less than stellar, her hypothesis that great-grandmother's house is slowly eating her alive. And though she hasn't allowed herself to contemplate the thought fully, she wonders if the house has eaten Chloe, too. She wouldn't put it past the place to do such a thing.

Roman says again, Let's go look. He wants to help her look inside the house for any clues about Chloe's whereabouts. He doesn't tell her that houses don't eat cats and people. Cora appreciates that, which is perhaps why she agrees to let him accompany her through the sunroom, into the kitchen and living room, and down the hallway to the back bedrooms. She gives him the tour, starting with where she's been sleeping to wait for Chloe. He says that makes good sense. The dolls, the pictures, the dishes, the papers, all ready for packing but seeming a little disorganized at the moment. The bathroom, relics of Cora's dissolution, children's books in piles all around. Cora says obviously she still has a lot of work to do. He says, You'll get it done. He picks up the book about Daffy Duck in space and they laugh at the absurdity. Cora tells him she has a confession to make, that she had actually seen the film *Fitzcarraldo* when she rented it but had forgotten much of it and wanted him to be impressed with her movie choices. He smiles and tells her every good friendship starts with a white lie and bravado. She admits that she's been watching *Fitzcarraldo* over and over because it's the only thing that makes her feel less lonely. He can think of no better way to spend the time.

Afternoon worms its way into the day while Cora and Roman talk on the back steps. Cora wants him to keep distracting her, perhaps she'll never want him to stop. His remarks on the ending of Camus' *The Stranger* turn her intimation into belief even as she scans the lawn for signs of Chloe. She will always want his thoughts on the next novel or work of art, will always want to hear the words he uses to describe a particular vocal inflection or the color palette in so-and-so's cinematography. She knows herself as fact on a sunny afternoon, loves how his hands conduct the symphony of his voice. He could never be abstracted, never be reduced, and even if he could, she wouldn't want to do it. Besides, she could never think of the right words. Tears well again in Cora's eyes but she catches them just in time.

Cora's body suddenly tells her that she hasn't eaten in a very long time, nothing but a little bread, a few snacks, some nibbles of pizza. She asks him, with boldness of attack, Are you hungry? Want to go find some food? Yes, how about the burger place down the street? Perfect. They walk together, still calling for Chloe. They arrive and order and sit and talk and eat. Cora eats her entire meal, perhaps too quickly. Roman's stories make her laugh between bites, give her new things to think about, new phrases to devour. If Chloe weren't missing, Cora might even, in this moment, describe herself as happy.

Roman asks with absolute nonchalance whether Cora has a job, out of interest. Yes, I have a job. Most people would find it boring but I am actually in love with it. Roman wants to know more so Cora allows herself a monologue. My job title is Abstractor. Isn't it such a wonderful thing to be called? The basic process: read a full transcript of some Congressional hearing, figure out what it's saying with precision and accuracy, condense every ten pages of text into a phrase of no more than ten words. Cora enters the confessional and describes her sins against language. She puts words in their places despite protestations, she dominates in ten words ideas that should take ten thousand, she forces them into perfect order when they want to be a ragged mess, she reduces complexity to mere play and verbosity to algorithmic formulas that only she understands but that mostly include subtraction and division, she acts out fantasies of vengeance, victimizes words that displease her, watches them beg for mercy, she hands out sentences like a cruel judge. She admits she has a flair for the dramatic. Smile. Laugh. He agrees and says she understands language down to its molecules, even its atoms!

Something about the atomic structure of language initiates a systems failure in Cora's imagination. Her thoughts turn to the house, to Chloe, to her hair and her skin. Perhaps, perhaps. Inhale. Exhale. Perhaps the house also calls itself Abstractor. She is its oblivious words in the process of being condensed, re-organized, truncated, compressed. Perhaps she's too bloated to fit in the margins so something had to go, the house finally had to get ruthless. Is this what it feels like to be abstracted? Cora sees herself into the future as a transparency, a few dusty trinkets left untended on the carpet. The house. The house is a terrible abstractor. It's omitting the most crucial parts, summarizing the wrong pages! How dare it deem Chloe superfluous! Cora's anger rises to her cheeks and Roman notices her silence. Are you okay? The world is a different color but Cora regains composure. Sorry, just had a strange thought. It's nothing. Roman says he should probably get back to the store, he's missed almost his entire shift and will have a little explaining to do. Cora apologizes for taking up his day and he tells her no such thing is needed. There's no other way he would have wanted to spend his time. As they stand to leave the restaurant, Cora's anger intensifies. The house. It won't see what's coming! She'll make a real mess of it if that's what it's been up to. Abstractor and Abstracted. How dare it try to give her a new title. She'll find a way to push herself outside the margins, to forbid it the satisfaction of a diagrammable sentence!

Cora drives Roman back to the video store and they talk about seeing each other at some point tomorrow. He'll be working, can she come to the store? Maybe during his lunch break? They could wander the streets some more together. Yes, that sounds delightful. What time? Five o'clock? Yes, I'll be there. Hopefully with good news about Chloe! She'll come back, try not to worry. Just give her some time. Until then, keep watching old Fitzcarraldo. He'll do to pass the time. Yes, I suppose he will. They hug for longer than Cora expects, wave each other goodbye. She tells him Thank you for today. He says, I'll see you tomorrow.

Despite her revelation about the house's intentions, Cora can hardly wait to get back. She's been gone a long time now and what if Chloe has returned? The drive back is full of Roman and the Beatles and Cora's realization that she still hadn't asked him about his novel. She'll have to write herself a note to ask him tomorrow. He'll think she doesn't care! Cora can't bear the thought. As the station turns to a commercial break, Cora attempts to fend off guilt for the day's laughter, the brief moments she had thought about something other than Chloe. Surely, she'll be forgiven. Surely, she'll be spared the worst! Cora's second thoughts take over as she pulls into the drive. Maybe she shouldn't upset the house after all. It's a wily predicament and she must proceed with caution.

The answering machine blinks its light out like a warning.

It's the first thing to catch Cora's eye. Always blinking. Every time she walks through the door. What do these people want from her? Julie is worried. Adam is confused. Susan is curious. The grandparents are annoyed. Luckily, they don't even know how annoyed they should be! Cora needs to face the answering machine with courage. Just let it happen. See what they want and then make a decision. If it's Julie or Adam, easy. Just tell them about Chloe. They'll have to understand. The grandparents, though, are a bit more tricky. A quick survey of the scene provides Cora with confirmation of their future dissatisfaction. What is she going to do?

First, she must press the button that says play. Such a barbaric word! If only it knew it would call itself something else! A scratchy message begins with Hello, Cora. A familiar, sweet voice. It's the grandparents. Grandmother, to be exact. Of course they would call at a time like this! They are concerned. They haven't heard from Cora and are getting worried. They've decided to move up their arrival to the day after tomorrow. Cora sinks. The day after tomorrow! The dining room chair holds her isolated grief and panic. She can't leave! Not until she finds Chloe. It just can't happen. Something will need to be done, quickly!

Maybe the grandparents will understand Cora's predicament. She can tell them about Chloe and they will let her stay as long as she needs. Could that happen? Cora wonders and remembers that the grandparents had protested Chloe's presence from the beginning. She'd make a mess, she'd urinate on the carpet, she'd smell up the house. Cora had assured them there would be no problem, that Chloe is the cleanest cat in the world. But now they're in a hurry, they'd tell Cora to simply leave some food out and check back each day. It wouldn't work. Cora is at a loss. The answering machine light still flickers even though she's already pressed play. It's doing that to taunt her. She can feel it. Her body slumps in a chair next to a table cleared of drinking glasses. She cannot think how to proceed. Blink. Blink. Red light. Blink. A decision must be made. Cora picks up the machine with both hands, holds it high over her head, and smashes it with all her strength to the ground. No more blinks. No more light. No more voices.

The blanket bed and the Queen of Prussia call to her so she joins them in the sunroom. So tired. Maybe she'll just lay down for a few minutes to rest, push play on *Fitzcarraldo* and listen as she drifts. She should probably go to work tomorrow. Maybe they'll give her a few more days if she explains the situation. Her thoughts fade to images of newspapers on Susan's desk and Roman and postcards that long to visit the places pictured on themselves.

CORA WAKES THE NEXT morning to the sound of purring. Chloe has taken her place on the pillow and is nuzzling her forehead to Cora's. Chloe! Nose to nose, kiss, kiss, pet, hug, whisker to cheek, wet tears and purrs so deep they seem to hurt. Chloe, are you okay? Are you hurt? Are you hungry? Where have you been? I missed you so much! The reunion lasts until Chloe rises from the pillow and chirps out her demands for food. Okay, I know what you want. Let me get you a clean bowl. Cora brings the food out to the sunroom and sits with Chloe while she eats at the speed of panic. She purrs and eats and then returns to Cora for more hugs and pets. She turns her head and heaves to vomit on the blanket bed and Cora says You poor thing and scoops her into her arms. She checks Chloe for cuts and scrapes, for bugs and webs and splinters. She combs Chloe's hair with the brush they've used since she was a kitten. Chloe leans into the sensation with her whole body, allows Cora to clean her back and belly and tail.

The two curl up on great-grandmother's chair and purr and

talk and rub each other's faces. Chloe nestles into Cora's lap and falls asleep. Cora doesn't move, just lets Chloe sleep and falls asleep herself in the quiet peace of the living room. After an hour Cora's legs begin to ache but she doesn't dare disrupt Chloe's slumber so she sits and sits and cries a little out of relief for her friend's safe return. She's definitely not going to work today. She'd already be late and nothing could keep her away from Chloe. Besides, the grandparents will be here tomorrow and she needs to take Chloe to the vet to make sure she's still in good health. And she certainly has no time for the nuisance of seeing her co-workers today.

Cora listens to Chloe breathe and attempts to sort out her plans for moving forward. First, when Chloe wakes, they'll go to the emergency animal hospital. After that, the house situation will need some attention. The sunroom has already been closed tight, the television cord has been unplugged and left in the room, the kitchen door locked to keep Chloe inside. She'll need to clear out the garbage and Chloe's vomit before the grandparents arrive. Cora looks around to determine the best way to handle the rest of the rooms in the house. There is just so much to do and no time to do it! The grandparents will be furious with her. Julie and Adam will be furious, Susan is likely already furious now that she's another abstractor short for this month's issue. Doesn't everyone know that Chloe has returned and that makes all the difference? Cora supposes no one really cares. Except Roman. If only some brilliant strategy could stop them all from feeling their emotions! Cora doesn't get mad at *them* so what gives them the right to get angry with her? It's an injustice, an unequal measure Cora cannot set back to balanced.

Chloe wakes and wants more of her morsels and gravy. Cora sits with her, then puts a soft blanket inside her carrier for the drive to the hospital. Chloe mews the whole way in small whines and Cora says It's okay, Chloe. It's okay. In the office and all through the visit, Chloe clings to Cora. Cora clings back. The doctor examines her, takes her temperature and weight, checks her eyes and teeth and heart and lungs and feels her abdomen. Cora strokes Chloe's head during the investigation and approves a few precautionary measures in case she picked up fleas or a parasite while she was outside. Chloe will be okay so Cora will be okay.

The car is filled with worry on the way back to great-grand-mother's house. Cora still doesn't know what to do. One decision has become clear over the past hours with Chloe: they cannot stay at the house for one day longer. The grandparents are practically on their way and Cora can't risk the house exacting further vengeance on her or especially on Chloe! Chloe, let's give the house some space, okay? Maybe it can recover its senses, regain its bearings after the loss of great-grandmother. It's as lost as you and I, Chloe. Just as lost.

They'll leave today. Now, in fact. But to where? And what about Chloe? Maybe she should stay a little while longer just to let Chloe have some time in comfort with the dolls and the sofa and water everywhere for her to drink. But then what? Someone else's house? Why hadn't she just tried in earnest to find an apartment? It's no use regretting that now, Chloe. We need to think of somewhere to go. Julie's unlit basement with no windows for Chloe and Julie's demands and voice and dirty dishes? No way. Adam is out of the question. His place is much too clean and could we stand to look at those eyebrows for a single second more? Besides, they'd both want things in return that we just don't want to give, do we Chloe?

We'll just need to go alone. Just the two of us. We have money. We've been saving this whole year thanks to the free rent. Do you think it's stealing? We didn't exactly finish the task they set out for us, did we, Chloe? We could leave them the money on the dining room table. That might make them at least a little less angry. Show that we're responsible and considerate and that we acknowledge the need for penance. But Chloe, we'll need that money. Your prescription food alone is more than we can manage! Maybe we should just keep driving north as far as we can go. We could find a pretty college town and a little place to live and work at a little job with no consequence. Or maybe a big city where we can use our degree in the humanities to some humanitarian purpose. Maybe we should find somewhere in the middle where we can become anonymous and unknown. We could keep driving west as far as we can go! That's something people do, isn't it, Chloe?

The radio tunes itself to Cora just before pulling into great-grandmother's driveway. Mean Mister Mustard sleeping in the park and shaving in the dark to save paper. Cora and Roman had laughed about the words yesterday in the car and then both sang along for a lyric or two. Do you think we'll see him again, Chloe? Maybe he's better off without us anyway. We don't want to admit it, but Chloe, the world isn't an abstract. We can't put it all in its perfect place no matter how hard we try. The words always escape the margins! And maybe we wouldn't *want* him in the margins. Did you ever think of that,

306 / SARAH D'STAIR

Chloe? It occurs to Cora that Chloe hasn't met Roman and decides the fact is further evidence that the world puts in a lot of effort not to make any sense.

Wait here for me, Chloe. I'll be right back. Cora rolls down the windows in the car so Chloe can feel the breeze. I just need to get a few things from inside the house. As soon as she walks in the door, Cora is met with faces that beg her not to leave. The little doll who stayed with her in the sunroom, the women who wink and smile, the sad bratty girl who is as known to Cora as her own self. Faces of dishes and papers. Faces on albums and gadgets and boxes and uncomfortable chairs. Faces of carpet and dust and dining room table. Faces of broken pieces on a kitchen floor and faces of the letters that fill a dozen scraps of paper.

I'm sorry, I can't think about any of you right now. I need to go. I'm sorry. I'm so sorry! Cora begins her preparations. She goes to the back of the house and puts a few of her least hated clothes into the small suitcase she brought when she first arrived. Jeans, a few t-shirts, underclothes. She has no need to impress anyone with her appearance. In fact, no one she knows will be looking at her at all, a small turn of fortune in an otherwise sad situation. Next, she packs Chloe's necessities: litter box, litter, toys, water bowl, food bowl, the wet and dry prescription food. She'll need to find somewhere new to buy Chloe's food but she'll think about that later.

What else? Cora looks around to make sure she hasn't forgotten anything important. Maybe she should at least rescue one thing from great-grandmother's house, just one small trinket or item that can be saved from its fate or the incinerator. But what? Something from the kitchen? A piece of clothing she might wear when she has the confidence? Maybe one of the pictures or one of the dolls? A book or piece of paper? Of course. Cora knows without a second thought. Of course! The little girl. The ugly little girl who torments and loves her, who has shown her the true face of melancholy. So lonely. So mad! Cora will find a way to make her happy but it will not be here at great-grandmother's house. She will find a way to make her smile, make her hair less disheveled and her raggedy doll less afraid, she will find a way. She promises!

One last thing. She can't believe she almost forgot! *Fitzcarraldo*. Remember? She had promised never to return it and can't leave it here just to have someone make the mistake of sending it back. That would be terrible! Cora sneaks into the sunroom and tries her best not to disturb the still depressed air. Presses eject. Slips the tape into its case and locks the door behind her.

Cora ferries her suitcase and Chloe's essentials out to the car, making extra sure to account for her wallet and keys. All she needs in the world is now with her in the car. Chloe, I think that's it. Is that it? Chloe looks at her through the carrier door and mews. Yes, I know there's so much left in the house. But we can't take it all with us. That'd be both impractical and impossible. Mew. Chirp. It's sad, yes! Pet pet through the carrier door. They'll just need to survive on their own. They'll find a way, we hope. Mew. Chloe, we can't save them all! Chloe slow blinks and puts down her head for a rest.

It's time to go. Where, you ask? I really don't know, Chloe, but we'll figure it out. In the meantime, I promise you won't have to stay in that carrier for long. I'll sneak you into a hotel somewhere sometime soon. Promise! Cora starts the car and turns down the radio, feels the breeze on her cheek from the open window. As she puts the car into reverse, one last moment of clarity reminds her what she needs to do. Wait for me, Chloe. I'll just be a second! She turns off the car and removes great-grandmother's key from the keyring, walks it back into the house and leaves it on the dining room table. She locks the door on the way out. There's no going back now! Chloe, that's it. Only one direction left to go.

Cora stays in the car for a minute longer and turns up the volume once again. She wonders if the station will last forever, wonders where she'll be at five o'clock tonight. As the car finds its way onto the street, she wonders about those Mormon Crickets she'll never get to know, tells Chloe maybe one day they might get to hear them singing.